Dead
Lift

~~by~~

PETER D. BOVÉ

Published by Taxicab Press, Montauk, NY

TaxiCabPress@gmail.com

Printed in the United States of America.

Edited by Lily Yarders-Brenner

Cover design by Alysa Choudri

ISBN 10: 1979003467 ISBN 13: 978-1979003469

DEDICATION

To Saint Augustine, whose work, 'Confessions', allowed me to believe in the potential virtue of this book.

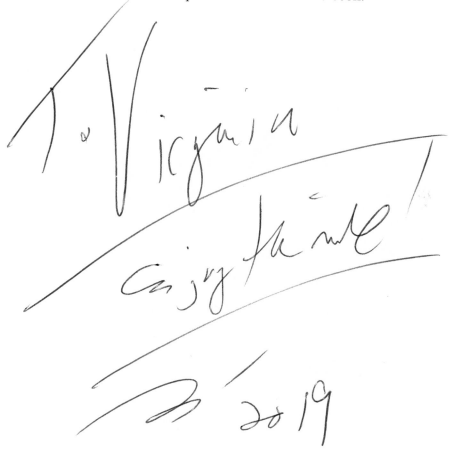

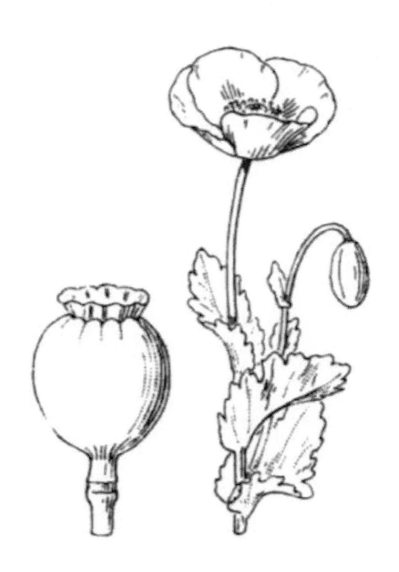

CONTENTS

ACKNOWLEDGMENTS

Warmest and heartfelt thanks to Lily, who showed
me more patience than I had any right to expect.
I consider it a true privilege to have been the recipient
of her brilliant and tireless editing.
Le merci cent fois du fond de mon coeur!

A warm thanks to Surf Lodge for the Wi-Fi.

For the attentive ear, informed mind and great pours
of James the Bartender.

And for Uncle Coe, may he rest in peace.

PROLOGUE

New York City, Hollywood and New Orleans.
It is the 1980's.

I

Heaven Looms

"Does it beseem thee to weave cloth of devil's dust instead of true wool?"
CARLYLE: Miscellanies, IV: Dr. Francis (1843)

Not unlike a child about to touch his first dead bird found on the sidewalk, Frankie undoes the tape and opens the tiny, waxed bag. There is a red star made from an ink stamp on it. The image of the star is smeared where someone had scotch taped the bag shut while the ink was still wet. Seated on the toilet, he empties the contents onto the shiny white Italian tiles that surround the porcelain bathroom sink. A distinct acidic odor invades the many wisps of perfume that swirl around the ultra-feminine bathroom in which he finds himself. He thinks for a moment how unlike his own bathroom this one is, the contrast almost beyond measure, when his mind goes to her, to Baby Doll. He knows she's just down the hallway in her bed waiting for him. He feels the excitement and apprehension as he slowly unravels the second of four tiny bags that he's set aside. Again the feeling emerges, like the child holding a stick about to make contact with the bird. Will it fly if I touch it?

A scene runs through his mind of the inconspicuous little pool hall on West 20th Street, where he scored that afternoon. The tall Puerto Rican woman in black leather pants and spiked heels, the way she leaned on her pool cue, and the stares he had gotten as he walked past two

5

greasy men and the only pool table in the place, right up to the small Plexiglas window near to where she was standing, like he'd been there a hundred times before. A ploy he thought necessary if he were to blend in and achieve his goal. He stuffs five twenty dollar bills through the small rectangular opening that had been cut out of the Plexiglas just above the counter he had eyed even before he got within ten steps of it. Frankie can feel her eyes still on him as she leans against the worn brown fake wood paneled wall smoking a cigarette. He'd never scored here before and had been warned that an introduction was needed to do so. He'd walked by a few times and peeked in just yesterday. It looked like any small Latino social club with a pool table stuck in the middle taking up too much room, while a bunch of misplaced characters from a Sam Peckinpah film hung around spitting on each other, shouting their conversation. But there was something else. A sign... a notion... a sixth sense told him, although in a very unlikely part of town, it was exactly what he was told it was.

He looks the large unkempt man behind the small makeshift counter in the eyes in an attempt to hide his nervousness. The man blows a puff of cigarette smoke in Frankie's direction. Half of the smoke flows towards him through the small holes that someone had drilled in the Plexiglas window. The rest bounces back towards the man's face, swirling around his head, giving him the appearance of a fat lazy fire dragon. He ruffles the money between his huge slumberous fingers, like five dried leaves, and stares Frankie down. Frankie feels as though the man might at any moment blow a breath of fire onto the bills, turning them to ash. A still and reckless silence holds the room, as he looks Frankie up and down. The dragon is waiting for him to say something and Frankie knows it. He continues rubbing the dried up rumpled leaves which used to be Frankie's money between his large round deeply creased fingers. Fingers that appear to be increasing in size by the second, and stares Frankie down some more. Frankie can sense the woman still watching him, and now the two men she was shooting pool with, also. He can hear occasional whispers between them, more like grunting sounds, but the thing about them he notices above anything else is that they have stopped playing pool. He is doing his best to ignore the feeling of being watched when the fire dragon, now of enormous proportions, tosses his money aside. Then after the longest three seconds in the world, he gives Frankie a knowing smile and slowly slips a bundle of tiny, waxed bags through the small opening, wrapped tightly in the thinnest green rubber band Frankie has ever seen.

Frankie palms the bags, relieved. He doesn't even count to make sure there are ten. 'There must be...' he thinks to himself. He also knows that if there aren't, there's nothing he would or could do about it. He stuffs his hands in the pockets of his leather jacket unceremoniously and turns around slowly. He doesn't feel comfortable making any sudden gestures. He looks over at the two men near the entrance, then at the pool table. He completes his turn to glance over at the tall Puerto Rican woman still leaning against the wall checking him out. The thought that he might not get out of the place with his precious cargo flashes through his mind when the tall Puerto Rican woman gives him a droll, suddenly friendly, smile. She stamps her cigarette out on the linoleum floor, takes a step towards the pool table, leans over, and carefully, with great skill, cracks the cue ball into the nine ball making a long difficult bank-shot the length of the entire table into the corner pocket nearest to where Frankie is standing. The two men at the other end of the pool table protest in disbelief. She looks up at Frankie and smiles, raising her eyebrows. Seated in the bathroom now he can't help but think back to her. The way she leaned on the pool table after making that incredible bank-shot, looking up at him with that coy smile that seemed to say, 'don't you wish you were me, eh gringo?' But especially her large dark olive skinned breasts, as they were merely inches away from him just this afternoon, barely contained in her tight black leather bustier, a size too small, beckoning, when there is a knock on the bathroom door.

"Are you okay in there?" Baby Doll asks, in her girl-like voice and accommodating manner.

"Yeah... fine... be out in a minute," Frankie answers.

Its snowy white sheen glistens, as the heroin's flake-like quality causes the otherwise powdered substance to stick to the surface of the sink. Frankie notices a short pubic hair near to where he had emptied the contents of the four bags. With a moistened fingertip he carefully takes hold, flicking it from his fingers between his legs into the toilet. Everything that happens now until he does it is pure ecstasy.

These are the fleeting moments he cherishes. Like the moments between betting on a horse race, the gates bursting open and the horses struggling for that early position. Or the seconds between deciding to dive into the cold north Atlantic and the moment that instant chill of the icy water hits his face and body as he streams beneath the waves. These are the moments he loves. He seeks, actually... the elusive moments between decision and actual event. It becomes an event of its own that he celebrates ...if only by his recognition of it in direct contrast to the decision or actual event itself.

Why not the moment of conquest or discovery? No, it is the moment of anticipation ignited with imagination that most excites Frankie. Will the bird fly if I touch it?

He inhales the heroin with a crisp bill rolled into a small cylinder. The familiar pungent vinegary taste expands from his nose into his mouth. The details go in and out of focus as he sniffs strongly, inhaling it all. He sits back on the toilet in a half smile, laughter gurgling up uncontrollably in him. All this sneaking around has him about to jump out of his skin from pure pleasure. He soaks a wad of scented toilet paper with warm water from the faucet. He lays his head back, places the tissue up to his nose and sucks the water into his nostrils making sure all the heroin gets inside him. The sensation triggers an instant feeling of relief strangely mixed with a rare form of pleasurable anxiety. He stares at the ceiling and sniffs as he waits for his nostrils to clear enough so none will drip out. He sits there for a moment with his eyes closed, listening for the kettle he'd placed on the stove to whistle. He flushes the toilet and watches the tissue, the four tiny emptied waxed bags, and the lone hair spin into the abyss. He checks around the immaculate bathroom for any infractions he may have left behind before switching off the light and opening the door.

The dark hallway swallows him up then spits him out into the large living room. The thick carpeting under his bare feet comforts as he stands there for a moment, looking out of the long row of floor-to-ceiling windows that run the length of the north and west walls, from the fireplace over to where the piano is. He takes in the huge thirtieth floor view of Manhattan; a massive twinkling of multi-colored lights, shiny metallic office buildings, beyond them the George Washington Bridge and the lights of passing boats shimmering on the water of the Hudson River. Baby Doll is out there on the terrace in a canvas deck chair waiting for him. She looks up through the glass door that separates them, and smiles, motioning for him to join her. He points to the kitchen. She nods her head then looks out towards the river, puffing on a joint. The kettle is about to whistle as Frankie enters the kitchen. He pours the steaming hot water into the teacup he'd prepared before going into the bathroom to snort up. The hot herbal tea will decrease the time it will take for the smack to hit him. He can already feel it taking effect as he takes a sip. He walks through the living room towards the terrace, tea in hand, thinking about the remaining bags left from the bundle. It is a comforting thought knowing he has wake-up bags. He steps onto the terrace, completely relieved, maybe a little triumphant at the thought, gloating even...

The sounds of the city from Broadway and Eighth Avenue rise up on a cool breeze that washes over him. He can feel it flow from his legs to his face. It cools the sweat that had developed on the small of his neck. He sits down beside Baby Doll on the matching deck chair. It takes him in. She smiles at him adoringly while he sips his tea and passes him the joint. He inhales the fragrant hot smoke as the world slowly grinds to a halt.

Without being sure of how much time has passed, or by what means, he's now standing naked in the bedroom as Baby Doll lies in bed. A soft steady breeze blowing in from the river plays choreographer to the silky white curtains that adorn the expanse of windows at the far end of the room. Her bed is a soft white satin fluff of cloud that embraces and caresses as he enters. They slide through it together, slowly... passively. Her body is firm yet soft... pliable. A scattering of freckles decorates her shoulders and back and, ever more faintly, her thighs. Their lips begin to kiss. Their arms and legs touch each other through faint reaches of energy not yet fully their own, mouths making wet various parts of the other's body. Frankie finds her nipple in his mouth suddenly. Slowly, gently sucking, he assumes a fetal position. His body pulsates in response. He licks and kisses his way down her soft warm belly. His tongue is on her thighs now, teasingly soft, relaxed and smooth as to compete with the layers of satin that surround them. Only the intent of his mouth will signal the obvious difference, as his tongue now seeks the various openings of her perfectly tanned body. She lets out a small sigh. Her long soft blond hair in his grip, while the delicate balance between pleasure and pain is tested. She moans as her body writhes in near ecstasy while his lips and tongue take turns with her. Then, without fully knowing through what fantastic bedroom acrobatics, he feels her warm wet mouth on him. Her soft tongue twirling gently yet intently around and around, up and down the shaft. His tongue and hers are speaking a new language quite apart from them.

He is inside her now as their pores open to the night air gusting freely through the large open windows of the bedroom. Her sweet ecstatic gasps for air rise up to him on crests of hot breath as he is mounted on her. Slowly, surely, spreading her wide, wider, until she releases a deep low shivering moan. A moan interrupted only by her heaving attempts at breathing, as her lungs search the thick moistened surroundings for oxygen. There are no longer two bodies or even one body. Now, there are no bodies, only dark wet electric drug-induced fuzzy images of pulsating flashing light sensations inspired by deep secretive impulses commingled with a symphonic thumping of murmurs, heartbeats and animalistic intent. Soon he will be asleep. Deep blessed sleep.

II

Fall Down

"He needs a long spoon who sups with the Devil."
Proverb, 18th Century

Hurriedly, Frankie runs towards gate #21 at JFK International Airport, the perspiration running furiously down the sides of his face, his wrenched gut riding four bags of Mr. D copped earlier that day. It isn't holding him. After a pre-boarding process that felt longer than it took for the Grand Canyon to form, Frankie boards the airplane in a huff. He knows something is really wrong. He should feel better than this. His mind races... 'Maybe I should have gone for the Blue Steel from that kid on Avenue B,' he thinks as he takes his seat on the plane, '...or waited for the Bulldog from Maria... the Dog never let me down.' His mind reels... 'Shit, I should've gone for the Dog! Or Red Star, but why bother thinking about it now, I couldn't wait. I had to make this flight. Shit! That isn't it anyway... the Mr. D is all right. Maybe I should have shot it! Nah, I hate all that needle and blood bullshit, I don't care if it takes twice as much to get off, besides somehow I know that, if I start hitting up again... this time I'll never stop.' His troubling thoughts continue as he takes the last sip of whiskey from his 3-ounce flask... 'That's definitely not what's wrong anyway, but wait, maybe it is... maybe I should just hit it up. Agh shit! Screw it! But, why isn't it holding me? Man! It's much too soon to be feeling like this! This badly... maybe it was the count? Yeah, the count was probably low... I probably only did two bags thinking I did four, so I don't feel like four bags, I only feel like two, which, relatively speaking, is actually less than two because I think I should feel like four bags when in reality I've only done two bags instead of the four I think I've done, having only done two, instead of four making the two bags I actually did do, when I thought I did four, actually feel more like, maybe... one bag! That's it! That bitch took me! I knew she didn't look like a Mr. D dealer. All the Mr. D dealers have those dark eyebrows and that weird smile, as though they're all from the same family. It's a tight knit operation, a family thing. That girl was black! She had nothing to do with that family! Oh man! They should have authorized dealers, like when you buy a Sony. Maybe that piece of shit bagged 'em on me. I bet she did! I know she did! Shit! She bagged them. That bitch!' He pauses, crumpled in his seat.

It's not long before his mind begins racing again. 'Wait a minute... did she? I mean she was actually very nice, personable really. Oh screw that! She's probably a con. She did it. Why did she do that? Hmmmm...? Maybe she didn't...' His mind won't stop working, as the perspiration continues to flow from his face. 'Maybe it's the rain. Of course, the rain! It's the rain. Just like old Herman said. The rain... the rain always does it. It gets in there, drains the potency and dilutes it. I should've realized it when I bought it. And it wasn't even a full rain. It was a... drizzle! The worst kind of rain! I hate drizzle.

Slow, persistent, annoying drizzle. Just rain and get it the fuck over with! Maybe it was the drizzle… Agh shit!'

He makes several attempts to find a comfortable position. The perspiration continues to flow from him. He closes his eyes and attempts to calm himself. No good! He opens his eyes quickly. His brain continues to churn. He looks around at the other passengers on board. He considers the lives of each one. What were they doing this morning, for instance, while he was trying to score some dope in that miserable half rain? That… drizzle. He couldn't imagine anyone he saw on the plane with a remotely similar morning. 'Screw them!' his mind tells him, 'It'll be my last dope for a while anyway.'

It's not that he can't score in Los Angeles. He has a connection in Hollywood for a heroin that more resembles opium and is referred to as Mexican black tar. The best way is to smoke it using a method called 'chasing the dragon', whereby a piece of the black sticky tar-like heroin is placed on tin foil and held over a candle. When it begins to smoke, you inhale the smoke through a straw or a Bic pen with the insides removed. It's a bit mellow for Frankie's taste, but if he did enough, it was okay. But this is it. He's quitting. He has to clean out. That is, after all, one of the reasons why he agreed to take what he feels is a stupid, worthless job that is beneath him. 'It'll be good to get away and clean out in the desert… the coast, yeah…' he decides. But it isn't long before his mind gears up again. 'Why am I on this plane? Where are all these people going? What do they do? Are they all doomed people? Agh shit, are we going to crash? Why aren't I in first class? Why did La Guardia have to be booked up? I hate Kennedy Airport! Damn it! I should be back in the city. I shouldn't have to go to LA now! Not now!'

It's pouring rain for a line-up of twenty aircraft ahead of the plane he is on awaiting a takeoff slot. Two hours of hell! Luckily he'd done this before. He had a pint bottle, the 16-ounce flask and a 3-ounce vest-pocket back up. They contained bourbon. He sucked down the remainder of the pint, most of which he pre-drank during the pre-boarding. The large flask has beautiful ducks rising from a reed pond carved on it and weighs a ton. He can't appreciate either feature, only that it contains 12 ounces of Jim Beam, ten bucks a quart. Who can argue with that? Unfortunately, they're gone in less than thirty minutes and it has now been close to an hour and forty minutes on the ground inside this stuffy, stifling airplane waiting to take off!

"Stewardess!" he yelps.

"Yes sir?" answers a somewhat curt steward.

"May I have a bourbon, please?" Frankie asks quietly, leaning up so as not to be heard by any of the other passengers.

"I'm sorry sir, the cart will be by as soon as the plane is in the air," the steward retorts.

"Yeah, only uhm... I'm not feeling very well, ...a bourbon would really help," he whispers.

"I'm sorry sir, but it is our policy to not serve passengers until we are nearing our cruising altitude!" returns the steward matter of factly, and obvious to Frankie that he has memorized it from a training manual.

"Yeah. But... I'm not feeling very well..." Frankie argues.

"I am sorry sir, I can bring you an aspirin if you like," the steward says with little affection.

Frankie looks at him with disdain. 'This is no stewardess!' Frankie thinks to himself... 'Stewardesses have pretty smiles and sexy legs... how did I get stuck with this good for nothing steward?'

"Get me a real stewardess for shit's sake!" He mumbles, half to himself, somewhat belligerently, shaking his head in anger.

"Sir, I am the steward here! If I cannot get you a drink, then no one else can help you. That is our policy... I am sorry!" he says, a bit short.

"Look pal, I don't need any ice... or... or even a glass. Can't ya just get me a few bottles of... you know... J&B or something?" Frankie smiles with as much charm as he can muster under the circumstances.

"Sir..." begins the heartless reply.

"Look, damn it!!!" Frankie yells, interrupting. "I timed it so I could order a drink by now! I didn't account for the fact that I would be spending an additional two hours of what is supposed to be a six-hour flight on the ground waiting for a drink! If I had known that, I would have flown to Miami out of La Guardia Airport, enjoyed cocktails the whole way down, comfortably... then grabbed a flight to Los Angeles from there. I would arrive at LAX at the same time and not have had to wait two hours for a STUPID FUCKING DRINK!" he ends up screaming at the top of his lungs.

The steward looks at Frankie completely stunned, as do most of the passengers in the immediate vicinity. Not a sympathetic face in the lot. 'Screw them! I need a drink damn it, and I'm going to get one!' Frankie decides.

"All right!" Frankie intimates, shaking but making an effort to calm himself... "I need it, I couldn't get to my doctor in time in order to renew the prescription for my medication, and it would really help a lot if I could just have a drink!" he yelps, beginning to raise his voice again.

"Ugh! I'll see what I can do," the steward retorts in frustration. He turns and struts up the aisle.

"You do that!" Frankie yells.

The steward stops, turns around angrily and gives Frankie a nasty look. He walks back, leans over inches from Frankie's face and self-righteously states, "I said I would see what I could do... if that is not sufficient for you, then I am sorry."

"No. That's good, very good in fact... thank you... I'll wait right here, great... yes, I will wait just right here for you... thanks... I think also... though, that... if I may? ...That... well... as long as you're gonna, you know...bring one, you may as well bring... six or even seven or ...eight... I mean they're such little things, those tiny bottles... in fact, you know, if they come in a twelve pack or something, I would take that," he says as nonchalantly as he possibly can.

The steward puts his face even closer to Frankie's face than before. "Are you quite finished?" he scorns.

"Yeah, I'll just, ya know... wait right here..." Frankie smiles... sort of...

Frankie is drug-sick scared to death of leaving Baby Doll, while his entire life falls apart around him. He can see it going, bit by bit, huge chunks of it simply tumbling to the wayside right before his bloodshot eyes. The last thing he wants to do right now is to leave Baby Doll and New York. Yet, he's on his way to Los Angeles because he was offered a ten-day location-scouting job he simply has to accept due to pure economics.

He left Los Angeles a producer less than a month ago, and now is to return, gulp... a location scout! You guessed it – grist for the mill. Even less needed at this particular juncture is an argument with a steward about a glass of whiskey, but that's where he is.

The head stewardess, Suzy by her nametag, arrives with a handful of bottles and a cup full of ice. She looks at Frankie mournfully as she places the items on the tray. The steward from the previous encounter stands dutifully behind her, grimacing and making eyes at some of the other passengers, who also look at Frankie fretfully, perhaps condescendingly. 'Oh well,' Frankie thinks, 'at least I got a drink.'

"That will be twelve fifty, sir," she says.

Frankie hands her the money and looks up at her. She looks at him and feigns a smile. Frankie has little idea what she's actually thinking. It's spooky as hell. After what seems an eternity, they walk away. Frankie toasts the last few people who continue to turn their heads and gawk at him. Then he gulps down some J&B. He pours in two more mini-bottles and, as he sips, his mind is free to wander to that morning again. It was a strange morning. It was unclear whether he was actually being offered, or was accepting, this job. His entire body was already feeling the results of heroin withdrawal, when the phone call finally came.

"Can you be on a plane at 4pm?" Maria asks. It was already noon...

"An assistant will be by to pick you up and bring you to the airport. Oh, don't forget your personal reference book, oh, and do you have any of that XP-1 film? We need that sepia thing... I'll get into details when you arrive." Frankie hung up the phone, half numb. Baby

Doll was already in the shower, nothing felt right. He thought 'I'm not even sure how to get from the airport to the Mondrian Hotel in West Hollywood, and they're hiring me as a location scout!?!' It wouldn't have mattered if he did. The pain, insecurity and self-torture created by heroin withdrawal is about to leave him all but incapacitated. He supposed some sick drug-romantic people would think it was interesting. He just didn't happen to be one of them. Not at that moment anyway.

The primary thrust of heroin withdrawal, aside from the intense debilitating physical pain, is that you completely lose your sense of humor. Think of it... you feel every physical, psychological, emotional, and spiritual pain ten times more intensely than you ordinarily would. While, at the same time, you cannot think straight, can't focus. You are at the absolute and dire mercy of your fears. Desperately unable to dispel any self-doubt or self-loathing with a humorous thought... a cliché... a double-entendre... nothing!

You can't think straight! Your brain is too busy being bombarded by your nervous system, which is in a complete state of disarray. There is no time to step back, find a funny point of view... step away and 'see' the 'humor' in things... There is no humor in it!!! Inasmuch as your brain isn't working properly, it can't see it. It can't, so you can't. All that exists for you then is pain, sorrow and remorse... ...and for what? For all the baggage, mayhem and dismay that was there the last time you fell over the coffee table laughing your head off at a funny joke or a comedy or the muse of a beautiful girl... or yourself. Especially yourself! Or is it especially the muse of a beautiful girl? For Frankie that question could not be properly answered.

Having survived the harrowing flight relatively intact, renting a car and finding the Mondrian Hotel in West Hollywood, Frankie is in his room watching 'The Simpsons' on television, jonesing off the heroin binge with a quart bottle of Jameson Irish whiskey ordered from room service, questioning why in the world they didn't stock Bushmills, and fretting how he's going to fake his way through this scouting mission.

He calls it a binge only because he quit the stuff last year. He vowed never to do heroin again. Frankie simply drank a lot of booze instead, which of course is like changing seats on the Titanic. In the past, when he was a bit more dedicated to the stuff ...before he quit... he would clean out by gobbling up every pill he could get his hands on. Stuff like Elavil, Placidil, Valium, Demerol, Percodan and Darvocet, all purchased outside the iron gates of Bellevue Hospital back in New York. Mostly mood altering drugs invented to keep the crazies in step. He sometimes wondered on which side of those gates he truly belonged.

Frankie would clean out from heroin this way every summer for years, taking handfuls of these pills, a huge bag of marijuana and a few bottles of Bushmills Irish Whiskey to the beach out in Long Island. Preferably the North Fork where there were fewer crowds ...and fewer parties... places like Greenpoint where he could find small mom and pop motels. The swimming pools in these motels were often less than appealing, but Frankie made it work. Other options included upstate New York, or New England in the Berkshires, where he'd find similar motels. Places like Craven's Motel on Route 22, which, at the time, Frankie was convinced was haunted by sexually perverted ghosts.

If it wasn't summer yet, there was always Florida. He'd just go lay in the hot sun until the shakes went away. Going to Florida was like pulling a 'Ratso Rizzo'. Rizzo was the character Dustin Hoffman played in the film 'Midnight Cowboy'. Herman, an old one-eyed junkie Frankie knew back when he was using regularly, swore by the logic of the Florida cure. Herman ended up on a chain gang on one trip down. He began feeling so good that he decided to rob a liquor store, but that's another story.

This method always worked, too ...for a while that is. A month or two would pass, when Frankie would decide that he could get high only on Saturdays. A week or two of that and the Wednesdays began to get shaky. So he decided Saturdays and Wednesdays were the two days he could get high. In a few weeks, it's back to the daily grind of scoring dope just to get straight.

There was always cold turkey. An approach that entailed agonizing withdrawal pain and puking into a pail kept at the side of your bed for a few days. That's how he did it the first couple of times. If he could make it past the three-day hump, it was clear sailing. Sort of... This trip will be different. Frankie is going to attempt to clean out while scouting locations, smoking grass and drinking just enough booze during the day to still be able to drive. In the evening, he'll drink himself to sleep.

Finished for the day, he plops on the bed at the Mondrian Hotel, pours himself a long whiskey and turns on the television. Bart Simpson is flunking out of school and can't manage to get his homework done. He's in his room kneeling by the side of his bed, praying like mad for enough snowfall to stop the world for a day so he wouldn't have to go to school and face up. His sister walks by and, seeing him, comments, "Prayer, the last refuge of a scoundrel." Frankie is laughing and crying at the same time.

His head is filled with thoughts of Baby Doll back in New York. Who is she with? Who is she screwing? Does she know he is such a loser? Did the play stick? Is he getting over or not? Frankie has decided that's what it's all about, getting over. Not letting anyone in on the big secret of who he really is... a loser! A no good, dirty, rotten, two-timing, self-loathing, frightened little boy... He knows that when everyone figures that one out, he's finished. The charade it has taken him so long to invent will disappear like booze at an Irish wedding. The finely crafted character he so carefully, yet mindlessly, created would stop playing the crowd. And when they run out of rotten vegetables, they'll simply leave the theater and find another show. The funny thing is, that most everyone is playing the same gig. Only Frankie doesn't know it. He just can't see it. It's as though someone said, 'Hey kid, break a leg,' and he believed them...

The desert never looked so grim. Nor did the Pacific Coast Highway or the San Bernardinos. Frankie is scouting 'Americana' for a perfume commercial, otherwise known as a 'fragrance spot'. He's barely holding it together to drive, as the world takes on nightmarish proportions. Frankie has the shakes, which not even serious booze is dealing with anymore, and his heart is breaking in a million places. Every song that comes on the radio causes him to weep and sob like a three year old. It's been five days since he arrived and his thoughts continue to churn... 'I should be feeling better than this! What am I doing? How did I get here? Where am I? What's happening here?' his mind demands to know.

Nothing feels right to him. He just knows he is going to completely screw up this job. He is thoroughly convinced that nothing he finds and photographs is going to work. He'll mess up and never work again. He just knows it. He drives around in a daze, guzzling whiskey and chain-smoking big fat joints, but nothing works. He can't dispel the beast. It just sits on his chest with a malicious grin, drinking piña coladas, laughing at him.

He finds a lone phone booth in the desert near an old cafe. He calls Baby Doll. He has to know what she's thinking. What she's doing... it's driving him mad as he imagines the worst. He knows it's dangerous in his state to call anyone, but he needs to hear her voice, get some support, ...some love and affection. 'I love you, baby... I can't wait for you to get back, baby... I'm so lonely without you, baby... I know some day you're gonna be big, baby...' that's what he needs to hear. He needs it desperately! Things were not that way when he left New York, so what in the world makes him think it will be now, is not the result of rational thinking.

He's crazed, a lunatic, and it reads like a book. He has to let the cat out of the bag. He has to confess. Practically weeping, he confides in her about the drugs and what's going on with the beast. He had to tell somebody! He needs a shoulder to cry on. She didn't have a clue that any of this was happening before he left, and she doesn't want to hear any of it now.

The phone call ends with, "Call me when you get back..." Click.

His heart drops, provoking his mind to reel in emotional turmoil. 'Call me when you get back? That bitch! Here I am dying a slow painful death of the spirit, and she wants me to call when I get back?' He needs love, praise, adoration, and affection: Lies! 'I can't talk now,' she says rushing to get off the phone... 'Ron Smiley, the Hollywood producer, is in town and my friend Donald is going to introduce me. I have to get ready... call me when you get back.'

Frankie is absolutely convinced that she's going to sleep with him. How could she just hang up like that? Leaving him standing there, all alone, to suffer through all this muck. He knows that there is little monogamous about their relationship and doesn't kid himself about it. He can't remain faithful to her any more than she can to him. Yet, the thought of her with another man drives him crazy. If he had the courage to honestly answer all the questions that welled up in him about her he... he... well, he didn't. The most significant thing to Frankie is that her appetite for sex and booze mirrors his own. 'What else is there to know? Who cares about the rest of it?' He figures... 'I'm no Park Avenue blueblood... what do I care? She's beautiful. Her strawberry blond hair always falls perfectly over her little round perfect face.' The more he thought about it the more he needed to see her smiling at him, laughing at his jokes and believing in every lie and fantasy he invents.

Frankie sits in the conference room with the shakes, sweating, hallucinating and wondering when he can make his move and get out of there. Nervously, he shows the locations he's found and photographed for the shoot to the director and clients. Everyone loves them. He's on autopilot and just because he doesn't know exactly what's happening doesn't mean it isn't happening. Everything is fine only he doesn't know it.

§§§§§

New York is a gray drizzle. He gets out of the red-eye flight from Los Angeles and into the backseat of the raunchiest cab in the city at La Guardia Airport, a fragment of a human being. It is wet-hot and sticky. He feels worn, unkempt and very lonely. As the taxi drives him to Manhattan he knows it is wrong to have returned, but he couldn't stop himself.

His apartment never looked so grim. He feels as though he's in a dream... a bad dream. His thoughts take over again... 'Why am I here? I should be back in Los Angeles finishing this job.' He could have stayed on for two more weeks. The producer had practically begged him to finish the scout and stay on for the shoot. But he had to get back right away. He has to see her. He needs a Baby Doll fix and he is determined to get one.

III

Cat and Mouse

"Please would you tell me," said Alice a little timidly, "why your cat grins
like that"? "It's a Cheshire cat," said the Duchess, "and that is why."
Alice in Wonderland (1865)

Frankie is anxious to get paid for the location scouting work. He's broke and a Baby Doll fix will be no casual affair, especially after his harrowing telephone call from the desert. Things seem more precarious than ever, since he made that call. How can he expect her to understand?

It occurs to him that we are always naked under our clothes, yet the moment we take them off, everybody freaks out. He has to find her and tell her about this! Meanwhile, one naked moment shared from a phone booth in the desert let the cat out of the bag. Now it's cat and mouse. Guess who's the mouse?

It is that very moment in the desert that flashes through Frankie's mind as he turns the key and opens the door to his apartment.

§§§§§

The old forlorn western style dance hall café that stood off the side of the road near Desert Mirage is etched in his brain forever ...a lonely place in the middle of nowhere. A few dusty cars and a beat up old pick-up truck sat out front. He walked in and ordered a double whiskey with milk. An old drunk sat crouched at the bar murmuring to himself, while a dumb looking kid slowly swept the dust around the floor. Like many things in the desert, the place is very large. He imagines that Saturday nights finds it full of giant cowboys dancing with giant cowboy women, getting into plenty of fist fights, while a few Indians sit in the corner laughing, smoking the loose butts, and sucking down the drinks left behind by the fighting cowboys and their giant dates. The bartender, who he supposed doubles as the waitress, leaned over near the register reading a magazine in between serving him drinks.

Frankie walked out into the Indian-hot sunshine, deliberating whether to call Baby Doll. He'd been holding back for days and was about to burst. She had no idea what was going on in his deranged head. All she knew was that he was going to Hollywood to work on a television commercial. An essential line of bullshit when you're in bed with a beautiful woman losing your mind, he thought. Losing his mind? He is losing his soul, and he knows it. He was aware of it then when he dialed her number ...that he had been approaching this very moment ever since the plane landed at LAX, that all roads lead to Rome, *cherchez la femme,* and she was the Pope.

The slaughter began even before she picked up the receiver. He was as the slave sentenced to the *damnatio ad bestias* featuring hungry lions in some lost century BC. After slaves have been torn to shreds by ferocious animals the crowd spills out to the bustling Roman streets on the way to an ancient drinking hole, jubilantly recalling the high points of the massacre. Frankie is deep in the belly of the beast, yet he can hear every word while being decomposed by the digestive juices of his own hilarity, except he doesn't think it's that funny. All the while, needing her as badly as he ever needed a fix of dope.

§§§§§

Frankie knows that most people don't ever get to this place, this point of hysteria in life. That there are actually people who manage, somehow, to protect themselves from these tragic calamities, this clinging to fading blossoms and falling headfirst into the gutter. Frankie just doesn't happen to be one of them. Not on that day, anyway. In fact, not for any of the days, weeks or years preceding the moment he turns the key, opens the door, plops down his luggage and collapses to the floor of his apartment, less significant than the hair on John Wayne's head. He crawls to the phone. It's too early to call, and he's nervous as hell, but he doesn't care. He won't allow himself to even think she might not want to see him. He picks up the receiver and dials her number. The phone rings. He hasn't a thought in his head. It's likely he wouldn't want any of the ones that would creep to the surface. It would be much too painful. She answers the phone.

"Hi baby. It's Frankie." he says, almost trembling from the effort.

"Hi Frankie. You're back?" she asks.

"Yeah… took the red eye," he mutters, unsure what she's thinking.

"I haven't been to sleep, yet," she says, almost nonchalantly. "Come over, I miss you."

'Come over, I miss you? What, is she kidding?' Frankie asks himself, completely befuddled.

Befuddled or not, Frankie knows this isn't the time to be asking silly questions. He is relieved, ecstatic, whole again. He hasn't even seen her, yet everything is all right. His twisted face takes on a smug smile, as a sudden flush sensation of warmth engulfs his entire body. It's the feeling he got when he was a little kid playing sick to get out of school that day. His mother walks into his bedroom to check the thermometer she'd left in his mouth exactly three minutes earlier. She looks at it, and says, "My poor Frankie, you stay in bed today, young man." His mom walks out of the room never discovering the heating pad he used to spike the thermometer, lying under the blanket. It's the soothing feeling he got when he was planning something truly mischievous, like the first time ever in his life he was about to masturbate. Or when he got a good hit of dope in the bathroom of a Japanese restaurant while his friends were all at the table ordering sushi. It's the expression seen on a cat's face, over its entire body, really, as it clasps the helpless mouse in its claws.

"I have a few things to do, and then I'll be right over!" he says.

The feeling comes as he hangs up the receiver, warm and cozy like a fire, a blanket and a good book, while holding out during a snow storm in a log cabin in Vermont, only it isn't.

He grabs a taxi to the production office that can get his check cut for the scouting work in Los Angeles. He still can't shake the feeling of being in the wrong town.

"Why didn't you stay?" asks Maria, sipping her morning coffee as she hands him the check. "Ben said he wanted you to stay."

Frankie looks at her and shrugs his shoulders. He felt, were he to utter a word, he'd break down and cry. He grabs the check and heads uptown to Baby Doll's. That feeling that everything is wrong begins to creep up on him. 'Not now!' he thinks... 'Not when I am about to get what I just traveled three thousand miles back to New York when I should be in Los Angeles making money to get!' It's the cat almost losing the mouse. But Wham!!! Down comes the claw to drag the defiant mouse back in. Sooner or later, that mouse will be free. Dead or alive is insignificant, when and where are the only questions. Questions he dared not ask himself.

Frankie enters her building, steps into the elevator and takes the long ride up to the penthouse. He walks to her door and stands there a moment He's biting at the bit and battling trepidation in the same breath. He can smell evidence of her in the hallway as a sweet feminine odor flowing from the door of her apartment. A heady mixture of perfume, incense and sex. He's like a wild animal sniffing the trunk of a tree. He rings the bell. He's still having a difficult time shaking the feeling of being in the wrong town, when she opens the door. The moment he sees her he knows he's in the wrong place. He can't do a thing about it either. He bends over to kiss her. She turns her head and gives him a cheek kiss. One of those kisses your aunt gives you when she doesn't want you to mess up her make-up.

"How ya doin?" he asks, holding her in his arms.

"All right," she says, absentmindedly. "I'm tired."

"Me too," he says nervously.

"How did the job go?" she asks.

"Great!" he says, "Great..."

He undresses and climbs into bed. As he watches her slip out of her white terrycloth robe, all he can think about is what might have happened with Ron Smiley. She crawls into bed next to him. It seems to Frankie that she is attempting to lay near him in bed, yet not have their bodies touch. They lie there quiet for a few minutes, trying to overcome their mutual uneasiness... soon it might be out of control and they wouldn't be able to stay that way, in bed together. Somehow, he knows neither of them wants that to happen. It's a point of departure. It occurs to Frankie that they don't really know each other all that well. He can sense her struggling to recall those moments of intimacy, trying to identify a point of reference as to why they are lying naked in the same bed together, as is he. They spar for a while, feeling each other out like a couple of heavyweights in the first round of a prize fight, before there was a Mike Tyson. Frankie nervously stares at the ceiling as the tension escalates.

"Why didn't you tell me about the drugs?" she blurts out, finally.

"I don't know, I guess I didn't want you doing any. I was ashamed..." he musters. He's becoming introspective about it. It doesn't matter though, because they both know what they want from each other. It's just a question of settling old business... forgetting each other's shortcomings and infidelities, so they can get on with the business at hand.

"How can I trust you now?" she asks, with what feels like borrowed concern.

Frankie feels like the mouse that almost got away. He has to conserve his energy, wait for the right moment of weakness. Play dead and wait for just the right amount of leeway. Then make a run for it.

"What do you mean?" he asks, testing her grip.

"You sounded so crazy on the phone. What kind of relationship can we have if you can't tell me about your problems?" she asks.

It was like Swiss cheese! He scuttles it into his little hole and begins licking his wounds.

"I'm sorry," he says.

"Are you still doing it?" her caring voice asks.

"No way, I'm through with that shit. I was going crazy kicking in the desert. It's a nasty drug, that's why I didn't tell you. I knew you'd want to experiment. But it's not recreational. No one understands that until it's too late. Don't ever do that stuff, okay?"

"You should have known what it would do to you," she challenges.

"You're right... I'm not messin' with that crap ever again," he promises.

A long pause follows.

"I mean, you kept calling me, I was busy. I had an important opportunity. I didn't want to be upset," Baby Doll explains.

"I know... I just missed you so much," he admits.

"I missed you too," she says.

She leans over, smiling, and embraces him. They kiss. Then lay there for a moment, silent. Frankie stares at the ceiling. The cheese is beginning to smell bad, and a few of the wounds are bleeding uncontrollably. But he is out of the clutches for now. He has broken free of the cat's deathly grip. He isn't free to roam around the house, because the cat hasn't budged from outside his little hole. He can see it sneering at him. But, he is safe for the moment in his little mouse house.

"Then, when you told me you were having dinner with Ron Smiley, I flipped out," he frets.

Neither seems sure what to do next.

"Did you make love to him?" Frankie blurts out finally.

"Yes," she says nonchalantly.

"You did!?!" Frankie asks, nearly swallowing his tongue.

"We went to his hotel after dinner. We were drinking and doing coke. We spent twelve hours together. He's really intelligent," she continues.

"I don't want to hear about it," Frankie interrupts. He feels like crying but can't. This is what he came back for. This is why he'd gotten on the plane in the first place, what he'd left a paying job for...

"Then what happened?" he asks, unable to control his desire to know.

"I blew his mind! I made him cry. He thinks I'll be a great actress."

"You made him cry? What do you mean?" he asks, not truly wanting to know.

As much as he wishes her only happiness, there is an underlying jealous rage brewing inside of him. He can't think straight. The things he wants to say and do arrive and leave like an express train.

"We were talking about heavy stuff," she continues. "He'd read 'The Road Less Traveled'. He was very sad," she says with a sympathetic understanding Frankie doesn't like at all.

"But you made love to him?" he returns.

"Yeah," she says.

"Great!" he frets.

"But I love you, daddy!" she says with unexpected jubilance.

It's like a cue. Suddenly her hand is on Frankie. Business is settled. Neither of them has anything more to say. He takes her with a near violent passion.

"Yes, daddy. Oh fuck me! Take me!!! I'll be a good girl for you," she screams loudly as they come together. For Frankie, it is dynamic, beautiful and, horrible all at the same time. He rolls over and it occurs to him that they hadn't used a condom. Finally they fall off to sleep.

IV

Baby Doll

"...So," shouted Julius Caesar, "The ides of March have come." The warning soothsayer answered, softly, "Yes; but they are not gone."
PLUTARCH: Julius Caesar

The most significant difference between a merry-go-round and a vicious circle is that you can step off one, while the other tosses you off like a bag of beans. It should have been a great lesson to Frankie, stepping off of a moving merry-go-round for the first time. He was eight years old. He grabbed the brass ring. It won him a free ride on the merry-go-round, but then he became dizzy and wanted to get off. As much as he pleaded, they refused to stop the merry-go-round just for him. The ride seemed to go on and on forever. 'Dizzy' evolved to 'nauseous' and he was determined to get off. He worked his way to the edge of the merry-go-round hoping he could slip off unnoticed. But when he got to the edge with nothing to hold on to, he flew off, landing on several people waiting in line. Then puked all over their shoes. He got a small taste of it then, at that tender age, how merry-go-rounds can often, and very quickly, become vicious circles.

Before he met Baby Doll, Frankie was desperate and lonely. Since meeting Baby Doll, he feels more desperate but less lonely. Things may not be improving.

Before Baby Doll, he would do crazy lunatic things. If only to challenge fate, it seems. Frankie was a lone wolf howling at the moon. His friends could always count on him to do something fantastically insane. It provided entertainment and relief from their humdrum lives, and kept them needing him.

§§§§§

One of Frankie's favorite haunts is The Crossroads, a tavern on Houston Street. Sunday morning often finds him there. It's ten am and sunlight streams through the large front window. Frankie is the only patron in the place. He's seated at the bar writing in his notebook and speaking with his favorite bartender, James.

"Daring adventure!" James the bartender states, nodding his head in agreement.

"That's right," Frankie says lighting a cigarette.

"Somewhere deep down, everyone holds an ancient, maybe instinctive, need for daring adventure, if only for the opportunity to face and overcome one's fears. That's why there's television," Frankie says with a wry smile. "At no immediate personal risk to ourselves, we can be adventurous, daring and heroic. In a sick way, it fulfills the need." Frankie insists as James pours him a whiskey.

"Most people are exhausted just from the effort of paying the bills, and become overwhelmed. Others are too complacent to pursue true adventure. A lot of people are just plain scared. Besides, there just isn't enough exciting adventure a person can make a living on to go around anymore," Frankie says, sipping his whiskey. "I believe that accounts for most of the mental illness in modern man. We're so close yet so far from real adventure, which, for the most part, has been replaced by fantasy," he continues.

"I see what you mean," says James.

"It's like cutting the balls off the family dog," says Frankie with a sip of whiskey. "We had a great dog, Hercules, when I was growing up. He'd run into my bedroom every morning, leap into my bed and lick my face 'til I woke up laughing and screaming. Then he began to bite my friends. The day he got back from the doggy hospital, my brother, sisters and I could see that he'd changed."

He rolls a cigarette and thinks back.

"Mommy, Hercules won't play with us anymore', we'd cry.

'He'll be all right in a few days. Eat your meatballs. Grandma made them', she'd say, plying us with our grandmother's amazing Sicilian meatballs."

"Grandma's meatballs!" James says raising a glass.

"And he did get better, sort of..." Frankie says, "...but he was never quite the same, y'know? And we all knew it. He'd peter out sooner than he used to, and tend to lose interest in us, preferring the floor to a Frisbee or a young playful kid hiding under the bed sheets," he says, lighting a cigarette. "He had no balls!" Frankie says absentmindedly, then immediately realizing the sad irony of it.

With a sad expression he meagerly raises his glass. "To Hercules," he says quietly.

"To Hercules," repeats James, equally somber.

A part of them wants to laugh, but they can't. They sip their whiskey in silence.

Frankie looks at his watch.

"Hey look, I'm going out with Baby Doll tonight. I better go rest up..." says Frankie, finishing his drink.

"She still wearing you thin?" asks James with a knowing smile.

Frankie rolls his eyes. "Like you don't want to know!" he answers with a sly grin.

Frankie gets up to leave, "Till next time pal."

"Yeah Frankie. Till next time," James says with affection.

§§§§§

That night, Frankie and Baby Doll exit a movie theater, happy and laughing. Strolling along arm in arm, they decide to go to the China Club and have a drink. At last call they're totally smashed.

The next thing Frankie knows, he's staring thirty floors down to the street below. He's naked and his arms are wrapped around Baby Doll's slippery waist. She's leaning precariously high into the air, her butt on the railing of her penthouse floor terrace as Frankie screws her wildly. He had just then nearly lost his hold on her slippery body and it jolted him back to consciousness from one of his blackouts. He shakes his head furiously from side to side in an attempt to get the blood flowing above his shoulders. Her face comes into focus. She's screaming wildly, eyes rolled into the back of her head. Frankie blinks his eyes a few times then looks down at the street thirty floors below. It looks very far away. He is quite suddenly forced to imagine them both tumbling to their deaths. A part of him is even tempted to let it happen. It feels as though he's watching it on television, only he isn't. He looks into Baby Doll's face again. Her mouth is hung wide open and her arms are thrown high into the air like a kid on a roller coaster, and screaming just as loudly. Frankie doesn't miss a beat. He continues to screw her, pounding harder and harder instead of screaming in mortal terror and pulling them both in to safety.

Despite his lifelong yearning for true adventure, misadventure is as close as Frankie ever comes to it. Perhaps because of this same unexplained phenomenon, he feels obliged to fulfill the distinct need in his friends, as well as everyone he meets, to be close to another person doing the things that they, themselves, would not dare to do. It's irresponsible, dangerous and costly. He's no hero. He's just a drunk... ...a well-loved drunk, however, so everybody eggs him on because he's very entertaining. Frankie thrives on the attention even though he doesn't fully understand it.

The next evening, Frankie and his pal Tim enter a bar on the Upper West Side. The Bartender sees Frankie and drops everything. "Hey, how ya been? Good to see you again. Bushmills, right? ...Straight up with a soda back." he announces proudly, above the din of the noisy bar.

Frankie hasn't even caught his breath, yet the drink is poured and sitting on the bar. The guy loves him! Frankie sucks back the drink without thinking.

"How's the film business treatin' ya?" asks the bartender, pouring Frankie a second drink.

Frankie gives the Bartender a quizzical look. He sucks down the drink and leans over to his friend Tim.

"Who is this guy?" Frankie asks. "It's a little spooky how he knows so much about me. I've never even been in this bar before."

"Frankie, we were here last week. Don't you remember?" Tim says, shaking his head.

§§§§§

Frankie has a small, seemingly insignificant tendency to spill milk wherever he goes. If you ever invite him to your home, be sure to hide delicate objects before he arrives. Crystal candelabra, wine glasses, mirrors, small pets, perfume bottles, terrycloth robes, anything white, most knick-knacks, valuable original works of art, pianos, guitars, banjos, Ming dynasty vases, one-of-a-kind hand-blown glass objects, Art Deco Tiffany lamps, and hundred-year-old bonsai are just a few of the things Frankie has damaged or destroyed, by accident, at one time or another in peoples' homes, restaurants and assorted shops around town.

Shortly after they met ...Baby Doll and Frankie ...he slowed down on the booze in an attempt to control his arms and legs. They apparently did things to piss Baby Doll off. Frankie often felt that he actually had little to do with her sudden fits of rage. Just the same, he was growing tired of never knowing when she would blow her top, and being unexpectedly asked to leave at some ungodly hour, just as sleep began to creep into his head.

"Get out!" she'd scream.

That's the thing that made him slow down ...for a while. He couldn't even remember what it was he did half the time. What Frankie began to realize is, neither did Baby Doll. He'd drip a little wax from a lit candle onto the bathroom floor.

"You have no respect for me!" she'd yell and cry... "You're always wrecking my apartment."

Strange thing is, a large part of him was always relieved when it happened ...alone at last. He'd leave her place and drift around the Theater District for a while until he could slide into a taxi, go home, and conk out for a few days. Then, before he could figure any of it out, there'd be a message on his machine from her.

"I'm sorry about the other night... You want to go to the movies?" Baby Doll's sweet voice would entice.

He discovered that she did a lot of psychedelic mushrooms. The whole thing began to wear him down. But then something would happen.

She had a lot of girlfriends. Sometimes they'd all end up in bed together. Frankie is but a man...

"I think Jennifer wants to come over," she'd taunt...

What could he say? Sex with Baby Doll was everything he'd ever dreamed of. Nothing was taboo, all was forgiven, everything explored.

Then Frankie begins to produce national fashion and beauty spots. He's meeting models like crazy but keeps Baby Doll far away from all the action. And, even though he's suddenly earning far better money, he can't keep up with the pricy distractions Baby Doll is accustomed to. The expensive restaurants, gifts and vacations are taking their toll. Half the time, he's struggling just to make rent. His credit is a mess. He owes tens of thousands in back taxes. Yet, he'll get his hands on a few bucks and blow it all on Baby Doll.

Questions continue to penetrate his fragile mind. 'Why aren't I at home writing the next great American novel? What am I doing? I'll never amount to anything. Who are

all these girlfriends of hers? Where do they come from?'
Yet the answers don't come, and nothing changes.

He thinks back to the first morning he spent the night at
her place. He wakes up and looks around, trying to
focus. The floors are finely carpeted... framed art hangs
on the walls ...perfectly level... large mirrors cover entire
walls... There are two huge Sony televisions, a piano,
leather sofas, a fireplace, and numerous large windows
as opposed to the few behind the stacks of books and
magazines at his downtown tenement apartment. One is
a sliding glass door that leads to her private penthouse
terrace. Everything is well tended. And there's food in the
fridge! Items that he can remember his mother bought,
but that he never thought to buy for his own
impoverished house, like strawberries and cream,
salami, Cracker Barrel cheese, turkey breast and
Pepperidge Farm bread. Frankie never bought that stuff.
His refrigerator was full of cold pizza, Kodak film, week
old ravioli and butter that smelled like the rest of the
fridge.

Forget her bathroom, it's like an operating room. It is
little surprise that Frankie's presence leaves a trail a mile
wide. Frankie is like Pigpen from the Charlie Brown
cartoon, on LSD riding a unicycle through a China shop
blindfolded when he went to her place.

They woke up well after noon and she says, "I'm starved,
let's have lunch!"

'Lunch?' he frets... Frankie is one of those people who preferred to have breakfast as his first meal of the day, no matter what time he wakes up, and these days it is often after three pm. It occurs to Frankie that he's too broke to buy lunch. He knows for a fact, because the night before he was wondering whether he'd run out of money before he got trashed enough to sleep, or not.

So he says, "I've only got about thirty five dollars."

"Oh, that's okay," she says, "I want to buy you lunch. You paid for the night on the town."

"Okay, where do you want to go?" Frankie inquires.

"Let's go to the Russian Tea Room," she says enthusiastically. "It's only a block away. We can walk."

All he remembers of that afternoon is that The Russian Tea Room was practically empty, nothing tasted very good, and he ordered a drink.

Frankie and Baby Doll never went out with each other's friends. It would have upset the delicate balance they've created. They didn't have any mutual friends, other than the rock star who first introduced them, and he was usually out of town somewhere doing his own thing. They have invented a little world where only they can exist. It is a magical place where other people didn't make any sense. He knew why he came. He began to wonder, 'why does she? Is it just great sex? No,' he thought, 'it has to be more than that.'

Frankie and Baby Doll are convinced that they are madly and desperately in love. They begin to see more and more of each other. Speaking every day. It's becoming very intimate. The subject of marriage would come up. They would lay in bed at night talking about it.

"I love you Frankie," she says in a tone that said 'against my better judgment'.

"I love you, too," he answers, unsure why.

"Do you think we'll ever get married?" she asks.

"I don't know. I just want you to be happy," he answers with a kiss.

"Would you come to my wedding if I was marrying someone else?" she asks with a sincere curiosity.

"Yeah, would you come to mine?" Frankie returns.

"Yeah, but I'd drag you into the parking lot and make love to you at the reception," she giggles.

Frankie found Baby Doll more beautiful than any girl he'd ever dated. People would often mistake her for Mariel Hemingway or Christie Brinkley, in restaurants and on the street. He knows that's the least of it. She is a Doll. A doll like Barbie is a doll. The Baby Doll reference isn't far off from the Elia Kazan film of the same title. Her pet name didn't come from the film, yet when Frankie saw the film 'Baby Doll' for the first time, while deep into the relationship, it made him squirm. He can't admit it, but there are undeniable, distinct similarities. He's ten years older than she is. She is wild by nature and nearly oblivious to just how sexy hot she really is. Despite all her sexual exploits, she's actually extremely naive.

In spite of her seeming innocence, she somehow manages many learned quotes about life, politics, show business, her family relations and friendships. These remarks always baffle Frankie. Where does she get these ideas? They definitely don't originate in her head. She's much too young to have that kind of perspective, and he's never seen her reading a book. There are sugar daddies everywhere. He just knows it. Frankie can feel their presence everywhere they go.

V

Licking the Dust

"He must needs go that the devil drives." William Shakespeare
"Therefore behoveth hire a ful long spoon. The schal ete with a feend."
Chaucer: Squire's Tale

A few months have passed since that harrowing phone call from the desert, yet nothing between Baby Doll and Frankie has really changed. He got back from Hollywood, they sucked up to one other, each for their own desperate reasons, broke up, got back together, broke up again, got back together... he knew it was silly, yet each time they would split up, well, each time she would break up with him, he felt it was the last time. They split up ten times in ten months. When you stay with someone out of sheer desperation, it's bound to happen.

One edgy morning on the way to brunch, Frankie spits on the sidewalk. They were downtown, having spent the night at his place. There is a tension building between them that Frankie can't explain. It rears its ugly head...

"That's disgusting! You have no class!" she exclaims.

Frankie is suddenly reduced to loathsome ...despicable.

"What?" he asks, unaware of what exactly she's referring to.

"You spit on the sidewalk like a homeless person. It's embarrassing!"

They get into a fight over it. A nasty waitress then adds fuel to the fire and Baby Doll refuses to see him again. He spends the next two weeks spitting everywhere he goes, every chance he gets. Then she calls and it's as though it never happened. He thinks he's in love with her. What is likely happening is that he is desperately in love with his idealized creation of her. She may be filling her shoes in the physical sense, but the rest is pure invention on Frankie's part.

When she breaks out of the mold for whatever reason, the whole thing comes tumbling down. Each time she refuses to see him, Frankie becomes morose, dialing her number just to hear her voice, hanging up before she can hear the whimpering coming from the other end, secretly hoping she would hear it anyway. It is definitive juvenile behavior, yet he felt helpless to change it.

Pain is the surest way to honesty. When we see someone in an honest moment, it is usually over pain. Often a person very close to them has just died or some other tragedy has befallen them and their heart is breaking. The next time we see them, it's as though it never happened. We don't reach that same level of intimacy with them. The distance appears even more profound because the need to confess is gone. Now they're fighting to protect not only pain and anguish, but their pride as well. Fighting for the approval of their fellow man, in this case you... your love and affection.

Frankie's dead broke again, not even getting work as a location scout and struggling at writing a screenplay, when a friend calls to ask if he can take his place and drive down to New Orleans with a film crew as a Production Assistant for the Super Bowl American Express spot. The friend was booked for the job, but suddenly got an opportunity to work with Jean-Claude Van Damme as a stunt man.

A Production Assistant would jump at Frankie's voice, suck up to him and serve him coffee not so very long before ...usually a bright attractive young woman...

"Is there something I can do for you Mr. Reno?"

"More coffee, Mr. Reno?"

"Oh Frankie, I took care of that thing for you..."

And now the tables are turned. Again... more grist for the mill... His ego is humbled, but what can he do? He has bills to pay, mostly entertainment to keep Baby Doll off his back and in his bed. Besides, New Orleans! He thought, 'Why not? I'll go chill out for a while...' He knows the work is essentially mindless. It'll be like a vacation. Aside from committing some unforeseen crime, it is his only prospect.

The night before the crew is scheduled to leave, Frankie takes Baby Doll to dinner at Flamingo East. She wants to go to Teddy's instead. They end up arguing about it. It never takes anything significant to bring on a serious sorrowful fight between them. Again he feels depressed... frightened... left out... alone... undefined... a loser! It's as though he's sent out invitations for every demon he's ever created to come dance on his face. They arrive from the past, present and future, dressed as fear, anxiety, longing, dismay, failure, inferiority, sorrow, and depression. They walk right into his life like they own the joint, turn on the stereo and start dancing. It's a party, and he's invited, only it's the last place in the world he wants to be 'cause it feels like he's in a demon disco nightmare and can't wake up ...only he's not asleep.

§§§§§

The drive down provides some relief. Hitting the open road can do that. Frankie is one of the production assistants driving the equipment trucks down for the shoot. It's a long trip by truck and he tells stories about Baby Doll to the other guys on the crew. It's funny stuff among men ...funny for the other guys, because they can laugh about it. Frankie's still in distress over her, but that's what makes them laugh. That's what's so amusing. But laughter's contagious and pretty soon Frankie starts to lighten up.

"Man, I love New Orleans," says Frankie affectionately.

"New Orleans, Louisiana!" adds Chip excitedly in his Southern accent. Chip is the oldest guy on the crew and from the South.

Frankie smiles. "N.O.L.A!" he answers.

"That's right! N'awlins!" Chip adds.

Most of the guys have never been to New Orleans before this and listen closely. Frankie loves an audience, so he keeps it going, Smiling, he says, "You know each time I come to New Orleans I get an instant hard-on!" The guys laugh. "I can feel the swamp breathing huge sweeping breaths of life from deep in the swamp muck. The air is so rich with water here it can't hold any more. If the air in New Orleans could carry more water, it would. It simply can't, and so it just condenses everywhere, leaving the essence of the swamps on everybody it touches. It's in everybody's eyes. You can see it!" Frankie insists, smiling. The guys are fascinated. "You can feel the air you breathe, your feet, your heart and soul all below sea level as you walk, talk, eat and tip the next stripper."

Chip laughs. "Tell it Frankie!" he says.

The guys laugh excitedly. Finally they arrive.

§§§§§

It isn't long before Frankie finds his way into a strip club. He sits at the bar with one of the strippers. She looks like Jodie Foster, only as Marilyn Monroe would play her, alluring yet innocent.

"Sometimes I'll just go to the mall and sort of look at people, then I write in my journal," she says.

There is a silence while Frankie watches, somewhat detached, as a young chubby stripper dances on stage, slowly removing her white knit top.

"I feel content sometimes to just gaze at the sky, ya know?" she says. Her eyes spoke. Frankie felt that she didn't have to.

"Sometimes I believe I can fly... up there with the stars," she spoke anyway. Frankie didn't mind.

"You can fly with the stars," Frankie says, sipping his whiskey. "If only in your heart," he says, looking over at her.

She shoots him a coy sexy look. Frankie thinks it incredible. Not necessarily unique perhaps, but remarkable all the same. It is the look he was sure she used on every hard-on that walked in the door. Frankie could care less. He was special! He was...

§§§§§

The last night in town begins on Bourbon Street, in the French Quarter. Two of the guys Frankie drove down with, Dan and the Midge, are on a quest to experience the magical delights they've all heard can be found on Bourbon Street. Aware of the disreputable pitfalls, they go. Knowing full well about the overpriced under-poured drinks and street flimflams from hustle-hounds, they go. In spite of the raunchy strippers smiling their untrue smiles in the deep hue of complimentary strip-bar lighting, the ones that always looked best after a few drinks, friendlier and more enticing with every dollar they manage to suck out of you, they go. In spite of all the grit-level evil manifestations this colorful sin-on-parade nightmare of queer meat has to offer, they go.

They are loose fish on a search for ecstasy. They're hooked!

Since it's their last night in town, most of the crew has already flown back to New York. The production assistants, including Frankie, are scheduled to drive the trucks back in the morning. They have money to burn and are desperately paired to this roaming moaning taboo enclave of self-joyous romp, known commonly as New Orleans.

For a young man, no trip to New Orleans would be complete without taking in at least one punishing blow Bourbon Street has to offer. These guys are the working class, after all. It's what they're trained to do, wherever they are. Bourbon Street is not even close to being an exception.

Dan meets some fat cat from the Bronx, and in a matter of minutes he's scoring coke in an alley behind a Lucky Dog cart; forty dollars worth of somebody's Sweet'N Low...

They venture on, entering an auspicious looking strip joint called the 'Orgy House' down on the edge of Bourbon Street. Billed as an X-Rated amalgamated fun house, as can be seen in the many photographs on display at the entrance. They walk in and are descended upon by the hostess.

"Hiya boys..." she coos, letting her fingers smooth across the Midge's cheek.

"How's about a private show, hmmm?"

They are like three idiots from the Midwest, suddenly. Naked flesh has the tendency to do that to a guy. She looks them over. Frankie knows they're being sized up. It doesn't matter. He knows that's part of the adventure ...although, misadventure is more like it. The strip club is swamp dank and very dark, with only the dimmest of red hues emanating from low wattage lights sparsely situated around the club, which is practically empty. A huge stage fills the center with a smaller one to the rear. A few uninspired strippers sit around looking world-weary. Frankie and the boys are the only customers in the place. One of the ladies forces herself to her feet and begins to lazily dance on stage. The guys order beers, and watch for a while waiting for something to happen.

"Want a private show?" a nearby female voice trying to sound alluring asks.

Frankie looks up to see a huge pair of breasts inches from his face. She is at least six feet tall, black, and beautiful in a vulgar sort of way.

"I don't know," Frankie says, speaking up.

"What is a private show?" Dan asks.

"You know, a 'Private Show'," she says, smiling and licking her lips.

"How much is a private show?" Frankie asks.

"Ummm, well for all y'all, or just you, honey?"

Frankie slings a challenging look to Dan and the Midge.

"What?" asks the Midge.

Frankie stares Dan down.

"What...? I don't know?" adds Dan, sounding uncomfortable.

"What d'ya think guys? I mean, c'mon," Frankie challenges.

"I dunno," Dan says through nervous laughter.

The Midge shrugs his shoulders, looking miffed.

"It's only thirty dollars for the three of you," she says.

"Thirty dollars?" Dan asks, a bit surprised.

"Uh huh..," she says, licking her lips and pinching her nipples.

"How many girls are there in a private show?" Frankie asks.

"Me an' her," she answers, turning around pointing to another girl seated at a table in the corner.

She waves her over. Now there are two girls at their table. They are cutting a deal. The hostess comes over.

"So boys, what's it gonna be, hmmm?" asks the hostess, in a voice that could've belonged to Mae West.

"What do you think? I mean... I dunno..." Frankie says.

"What do you think?" asks Dan.

"I don't care," says the Midge.

"You don't care?" Frankie asks, annoyed.

"I mean... I don't know..." says the Midge.

"I don't know..." Frankie says, mimicking the Midge.

There's a long pause. They all seem to be looking at the stripper's breasts, especially the Midge. The tall black stripper licks her lips again. Now the second stripper has her hand on the Midge's lap.

"What do you think? Yes or no, baby?" the stripper asks the Midge, as she runs her hand across his thigh.

"What the heck... let's do it!" Frankie says, finally.

"Okay!" says the Midge, with a sudden enthusiasm.

"Okay," Dan agrees.

The strippers lead them to a small stage at the rear of the club. The hostess drags three chairs over to the stage, and invites the boys to sit down. There is a wooden railing between the guys and the strippers. Not unlike a corral on a ranch, or perhaps more like a church pew.

The two strippers get on stage. A new song comes on with the volume turned up. The strippers slowly remove their tops, slap each other in the butt, feign various sexual exploits as they stick their tongues out, lick their lips and make eyes at the boys. The high point comes when the vulgar, six foot tall black stripper somehow manages to shove a Blue Tip wooden match into each breast nipple. She then snaps the blue tips to ignite the matches, which she lets burn dangerously close to her skin.

"This is no stripper!" Frankie exclaims, "This is a strip tease artist!"

She continues her erotic dance, squeezing her large breasts together, sticking her tongue out at the boys and smiling. "Fellas... we are witnessing a real actual old-school erotic dance presentation. A genuine show-biz routine, right here on Bourbon Street," Frankie exclaims, knowing he's full of shit and the boys probably aren't buying it.

The show wasn't totally unsatisfying, even if the routine was billed as something more than what it actually was: two especially raunchy women slapping each other on the butt, sticking their tongues out at them, while one of them set her tits on fire. The three of them spilled a ten spot each to see it.

They leave the club and enter Bourbon Street fifty dollars poorer, without yet getting their kicks.

They continue up Bourbon Street somewhat forlorn. "We're licking the dust!" the Midge says angrily, looking up at Frankie.

"Yeah," joins Dan.

Frankie can't remember having heard that expression before, but he already knew it well. And although he'd never admit it openly to the guys, Midge's words are pretty damn accurate.

Frankie stops and watches as Dan and the Midge continue up Bourbon Street. The Midge has his hands in his pockets with his back crouched over kicking a small stone off the crowded street, like a little kid who just had his football squashed by a train... and Dan is walking like he has a hole in his shoe.

"What? You didn't like that?" Frankie asks, trying to sound amazed.

The Midge turns around and stares at him. He doesn't look happy...

Dan looks at them both and says, "If any truly satisfying experience will be found tonight, it won't be on Bourbon Street."

"No, that's not true," argues Frankie vibrantly. "There are no rules to this game. It can happen anywhere, anytime. Let's not give up now!"

There is a pause among them as they stand in the middle of the roaming crowds of Bourbon Street.

"Okay," Frankie says finally, "maybe Dan is right, let's try something else."

The thought that he'd end up in some bar in the Quarter alone doesn't appeal to him in the least. Frankie needs these guys. He still misses Baby Doll. He's worked hard all week on this silly commercial, and since having the fight with her in New York the night before he left, she hasn't taken any of his calls. He is on an extended detour. He doesn't want to go it alone because then anything might happen. Besides, he knows, being the resilient creatures they are, that they will venture on in the face of all that dust. He, for one, has to.

At times like this, Frankie felt that if he were to call it a night and go home... First of all, it's unthinkable! Call it a what? Do what? Go home? It never entered his mind that it is even an option! He could never figure anyone that would 'call it a night'. What are these people up to? He'd argue. It's like calling a baseball game because of rain. Who on earth do these people think they are, night-on-the-town umpires or something? Frankie stands there in the middle of Bourbon Street muck imagining the scene.

"That's a night, I'm callin' it!"

"Whoa! Time out here fellas."

"Uh-oh... this could be trouble!"

"What's he trying' to do, Phil?"

"I'm not sure but... hold on a second... Holy Cow!!! There he goes!"

"Hey, he's called a time out!"

"Well Bill, I don't know what good that'll do, the umps have called it... I guess we'll just have to wait and see."

"He's running out to the end of the bar!"

"Oh boy! That's a confrontation, Bill. Holy Cow!!! He's kickin' up sawdust from the bar floor onto the bartender! Boy, is he angry!"

"Gee, I guess he really doesn't want this night to end."

"The players won't drink all night in the rain. They did in the old days, Bill... not any more..."

"It looks like they're gonna call it a night."

"That's it. They're all leaving the bar except Reno, he's gonna stay out there all night alone!"

"I just don't get it, they've called it. Everyone's leaving but he won't go home?"

"My God! He's just standing there at the end of the bar sipping whiskey alone."

"Actually, it looks like a double whiskey, Phil. I'll tell ya one thing, he's got a lot of spirit!"

"Either that or he's really thirsty, Bill!"

"Hahahahah..."

"Hahahahaha..."

"This is Phil Razutto."

"And Bill White."

"In New Orleans, callin' it a night..."

Frankie stayed out until staying out was over! Staying out was over because (a) he collapsed, (b) he convinced a young lady to go home with him, (c) he met a woman who could drink like he could and had a stocked bar, or (d) met anyone at all who had some booze and was as desperate as he was.

If he gave it up now, he knows sure as shit that he'd melt right there on the street like the Wicked Witch of the West. He has the strange yet absolute sense that he would mist up and drift away with the dark swamp air that hung low and still over the neon-lit corridors of the French Quarter. It is beyond certain to him that he would just hang there like an angry green fog trying to put enough solid weight back together to be able to enter a nice warm bar with sweet friendly luscious dancing girls inside, wiggling and giggling and breathing rich swamp air through sensuous big-lunged chests, inviting and enticing with smooth skin, soft and velvet to the touch and, and, and...

"Whoa, time out here, fellas!!!" Frankie yelps desperately.

"C'mon you guys! I mean, for crying out loud! What the hell? Next week you'll be home in bed alone, jacking off, wishing you were back here getting clipped for a few bucks to have a good time! It's here! I know it... I can smell it... There's a good time right here! Right now, damn it!" he says, standing in the middle of Bourbon

Street, glaring at the less than enthusiastic Dan and the Midge with amazement.

"We can't give up now! Not now!!! We've made an investment here. Look around you. Just look!" he states from the top of his voice, still standing in the middle of Bourbon Street, his arms outstretched, spinning around.

"What do you see?"

"Where are we?"

"Where the hell are we?" Frankie stares them down.

"I'll tell you where the fuck we are! We are in New Fucking Orleans! That's where the fuck we are! Right smack dab in the middle of the Voodoo French Quarter! Delta sin capital of the US fucking A!" A big smile comes to his face.

"We just got paid. Our pockets are bursting with per diem and petty cash. I mean, I'm ready to take the PC Express to hooker heaven and you, my fine gentlemen, are acting like you got pussy waiting for you back at the hotel!" he turns and approaches Dan.

"Are you holding back something I don't know about the room service at the New Orleans Sheraton? Because if that's the case, I'll just pack it up and go back there with you right now, call room service, have a little sent over and that'll be that!" he says, looking over at the Midge.

"At least I know I'll have a drinkin' buddy! Shit!"

Their quest forges ahead. Onward past the moaning sighs of club barkers, shrieks of small town adventurers, hot dog salesmen, and the wailing of Dixieland jazz, to the next, as yet unknown purveyor of carnal pleasure. They have no idea what is to unfold in this myriad of hazy bright-light detours from the much more ordinary world of cause and effect.

A short time later Frankie, Dan and the Midge exit a bar featuring a cocktail named 'The Hurricane' and traditional Dixieland jazz.

"That was ok. I mean, sure it's a tourist joint, ya sorta have to do at least once when you're in New Orleans." Frankie says. "But you guys are gonna love this next place."

"Let's find a phone. I promised to call Chip," Frankie insists.

Chip, like Frankie, a big fan of the oriental massage parlor, is back at the hotel watching the 49ers torture the LA Rams. Frankie promised he would investigate the oriental massage parlors in town and get back to him. Chip insisted he'd join them after the game ...that after a few hard sixteen-hour days on a film crew, he was primed for a massage, sauna... the works.

Frankie finds a phone and calls Chip. He listens a moment... "Ah... too bad pal. Maybe we'll see you later." He hangs up the phone, looking disappointed, and walks over to Dan and the Midge.

Dan appears unhappy.

"What's a matter, Dan?" asks the Midge.

"I dunno..." sighs Dan.

"C'mon! This place will cheer you up!" Frankie insists.

He hails a cab and they get in. "'Girls! Girls! Girls!' please." Frankie says to the driver.

The taxi rolls away stopping at a red light on Royal Street. It's quiet with the exception of some mournful bluesy jazz emanating from a nearby club. Dan jumps out of the cab without explanation.

"What's a matter pal? Where ya goin'?" Frankie asks.

"I dunno... I just have to be alone, I guess," Dan says. He shuts the door and walks away.

Frankie looks at the Midge. "You're not gonna bail out on me too are ya?"

"Nah... I want to see 'Girls! Girls! Girls!'" the Midge says, smiling.

"Then 'Girls! Girls! Girls!' it is," says Frankie, relieved.

They drive off through the fragrant streets of New Orleans. A few moments later the cab pulls up to 'Girls! Girls! Girls!' They step out and enter. 'Girls! Girls! Girls!' is right down Chartres Street from the Bangkok Spa and Body Rub. Frankie and the Midge find a spot at the bar and order some drinks. They sip their cocktails and watch an uninspired dancer strip on stage.

"You like her tits?" Frankie asks.

"They're ok," mumbles the Midge unenthusiastically.

"You ever go to an oriental massage parlor?" asks Frankie.

"No. You?" answers the Midge.

"Yeah, lots of times," says Frankie. "It's like nothing else in the world!"

"I never really had a massage, like ya know... anywhere," confesses the Midge.

The Midge, as Frankie affectionately calls him, is a chubby little guy from Pennsylvania somewhere. They only met on this commercial and, although they haven't known each other very long, I guess you could say they're pals. The Midge is younger than Frankie and considerably less experienced. Frankie feels it's his duty to show the kid a good time. Basically, they're just two men having a few beers at a strip club in New Orleans, there isn't much else to know.

"It's not just a massage. Asian masseurs believe in the complete release program," Frankie continued.

"Yeah? What does that mean?" the Midge asks, his curiosity kicking in.

"Y'know... a massage with a happy ending," Frankie informs him.

"Happy ending?" Midge asks, unknowingly.

"Look, you walk in and you get to pick out one of the adorable Asian ladies. They all kinda just sit around on sofas, you know..." says Frankie, taking a puff of his hand rolled cigarette. "Then, once you choose your masseuse, she takes you into a big wet room like a giant shower with water hoses and wash tables large enough to lie down on and she gives you a loofah bath."

"A what?" the Midge wants to know.

"A loofah bath. Look, you lay down on the table and she washes you all over with soap and warm water. And I mean everywhere!" he looks at the Midge and smiles.

"That sounds kinda weird," says the Midge.

"Not at all. Trust me it's a beautiful thing. Plus, there's usually a sauna or steam room in these places, too. Sometimes both!" Frankie exclaims enthusiastically, sipping his whiskey.

"Then you enter a private massage room together where she'll give you the most amazing massage you'll ever have. Some will even walk on your back," Frankie explains with great affection, as the memory of it washes over him.

"They walk on you?" the Midge asks, interrupting Frankie's train of thought with surprise.

"It's not like they walk on you!" Frankie answers. "They walk on your back... You never heard of that?"

"People walking on you? No!" the Midge retorts.

"What the hell do they do in Pennsylvania, for crying out loud? I mean... Look, let's put it this way... they understand what it is a man needs. It's very therapeutic. In the romantic sense..."

He looks over at the Midge. He isn't exactly popping out of his seat. But Frankie wagers that the Midge has had all the solitary foreplay he can take. He figures that the Midge has done enough watching for one night. It's time to take action.

"So, wha'd'ya think?" Frankie inquires, innocently enough.

"I guess it sounds kinda interesting," admits the Midge.

"Interesting? It's a dream come true!" Frankie declares.

The Midge laughs.

"I have frequented many an oriental massage parlor with my pal Buddy Ryan up in New York. It was a part of our weekend ritual," Frankie's voice becomes dreamy as he describes the experience.

"After much flowering attention in the loofah bath, administered by your hand picked masseuse, it's time to enter the sauna. I like to float between the sauna and steam bath a few times. When I'm in the sauna a little while, my masseuse will come in and relieve the heat from my forehead with a cool towel, or offer me a glass of cool water or some fresh fruit."

A gleeful smile finds its way to Frankie's face as he reminisces about the flowering attention. The Midge perks up a bit.

"Then what?" he asks.

"It only gets better from there," Frankie continues.

"Some of the spas have a whirlpool bath, which is especially important when you've suddenly decided that one girl isn't enough," Frankie says, smiling at the thought.

"Finally, at no rushed tempo, you'll find yourself alone with a beautiful, extremely accommodating Asian woman, massaging you like she's known you your entire life," Frankie raises his glass.

"Suddenly you are the beneficiary of thousands of years of sexually biased cultural pleasure." They toast.

"I'll drink to that!" says the Midge.

They share a laugh and order another drink. When Frankie reaches into his pocket to pay the bartender, he realizes he doesn't have enough money for a massage. He becomes introspective... "It costs a few bucks, but what worthwhile pleasure doesn't in this world?" he states with authority.

"Ain't that the truth!" states the Midge.

"Plus we have all night to kill, don't forget," he looks at the Midge and raises his glass. "And time flies when you're having fun!" They clink glasses. "In fact when you're in an oriental massage parlor, it's as though time doesn't exist!" Frankie thinks about this a moment.

"In fact, old Father Time is nowhere in sight," he continues. "Not until it's time to tip, that is, which, like most Asian skills honed by three thousand years of use, is accomplished quickly with invisible finesse. Father Time is quickly escorted in and out of the room. The visit is relatively painless and the cash falls from your hand like an old rag." Frankie sips his whiskey. "You know he won't be staying, so you don't mind such a short visit. In fact you barely notice. It is said that love is blind; sex is deaf, as well..." He shoots down the rest of his drink.

"That's all cool, but will she fuck me?" asks the Midge, taking a big gulp of beer.

"Will she fuck you?" Frankie asks with gleeful amazement. "Will she fuck you? Ha ha ha ha! She will re-fucking invent the meaning for you!!!" Frankie mimics the Midge, "Will she fuck me?" he chuckles... "You will not come out of there the same person as when you go in! That much I know..." He sips his whiskey, "Will she fuck me? Hehehee," he laughs, imitating the Midge.

He leans over and speaks into the Midge's ear. "She will fuck you until you drop!"

The Midge's eyes pop open. "Yeah, let's do it! I want an oriental girl!" exclaims the Midge, his excitement finally getting the better of him.

"Just one thing, pal," Frankie says, with a look of concern.

"What?" asks the Midge.

"Just try to remember, rugs are oriental, food is oriental, even a massage parlor can be oriental, but people are Asian." He looks down at the Midge, "I don't want you insulting anyone. You'll hurt their feelings, plus then you may not have a good time because of it."

"Oh... Thanks, Frankie. I didn't know," says the Midge.

Frankie reaches into his pocket, takes out his wad of cash and counts the bills. "Hey, how much money you got?" Frankie asks.

"I don't know, why?" asks the Midge.

"I want a massage too, but I don't think I have enough money on me," Frankie admits.

Frankie feels guilty asking, but is in a bit of a jam and must appeal to the Midge's generosity. He knows he's been generous with his knowledge of this little piece of underworld. Giving the Midge just enough to keep it thrilling yet still essentially harmless. 'I did introduce the Midge to the fantastic world of Oriental delights that can only be found in places like the Bangkok Spa and Body Rub,' Frankie's mind tells him. Frankie looks over at the

Midge, who looks back at Frankie a little suspiciously. But, after all, the Midge wouldn't be here, about to experience blissful majesty at the hands of an Asian masseuse introducing him to a world of ancient pleasures, if it weren't for Frankie, and he knows it. Frankie loves the little guy, but he's convinced himself the only way to survive his most recent fight with Baby Doll is to escape into another world, only he's broke. The Midge has known Frankie just long enough to realize that he'll work him over till he gets it. Even Frankie knows he has him roped in.

"I'll have it as soon as I get paid for this job," Frankie insists.

The Midge doesn't look entirely convinced.

"C'mon, you know I'm good for it, we're on the same job for crying out loud! C'mon, like a hundred bucks," Frankie looks at him, smiling.

The Midge reaches into his pocket and hands Frankie the hundred. "Alright! Let's get over there!" Frankie says. They finish their drinks in a hurry, leave the bar and go next door to the Bangkok Spa and Body Rub. They enter and the facility is clean and the girls look good.

"Well, buddy... what do you think?" Frankie asks, looking around.

The Midge doesn't respond. An Asian masseuse has him by the hand leading him into the back room and he's already out of earshot. The Midge looks the happy captive. He reminds Frankie of Lou Costello in that 'Abbot and Costello on Mars' movie with six-foot showgirls playing the Martians.

Frankie takes a solitary walk down the block to telephone Chip one more time and let him know the place looks great and they were going in, just in case he's changed his mind. Chip declines, saying he's too tired. He asks Frankie to call him when they leave the Bangkok Spa and Body Rub in case he gets a second wind and can join them for a drink, but Frankie knows Chip won't be meeting them. Dan was gone and the Midge is in good hands at the Bangkok Spa and Body Rub. There's nothing left to do but find somewhere to sit down and have a drink. He feels strangely drawn back to 'Girls! Girls! Girls!' and wanders back in.

He feels like a sailor, a merchant marine, or some other seafaring wanderer of times gone by, who just received his shore leave after a long journey at sea. It's a completely romantic feeling. The memory of the argument with Baby Doll back in New York is creeping up on him. Now that he's alone, it's all he can think about. Frankie knows he's in trouble. Seated at the bar, watching strippers dance on stage he compares them to her. Their bodies... the way they move and smile... the look in their eyes... their teeth and hair... their voices... hands, knees, fingers, noses, calves, breasts... he's a goner.

Mama Terry runs the place with a hardball edge. She's a fat runt of a woman with big red hair, whose only

concern on the girls' behalf is, 'do you have any money?'
And that concern due primarily to protecting her cut.
Frankie's mind wanders off to the Midge. What is he
doing right now? Frankie knows precisely what the Midge
is in for. He considers the fact that it's his first oriental
massage parlor experience. He smiles at the thought and
orders another drink.

To his left is a New Orleans police officer in full uniform
complete with sidearm, guzzling a beer and enjoying the
show. Not tolerated in places like New York City, it's a
strange sight for a Yankee, here it's par for the course.
Mama Terry can't be more pleased. Here's a guy who
shells out for drinks and doubles as the heat. She
doesn't miss a trick.

Seeing the cop at the bar reminds Frankie of his last trip
to New Orleans working on a Levi's commercial. It was a
901 women's jeans campaign, which meant beautiful
models... Frankie made sure the New Orleans shoot was
a party! They had rented an old carriage house in the
Faubourg Marigny, the next neighborhood down river
from The French Quarter. The old carriage house was
converted into a small boutique hotel. It had a swimming
pool with a hot tub where the horse-drawn carriages in
times of old once rode in, a few small cottages and the
main house. Every night during that five-day shoot was a
party. Before the advent of DVR, allowing viewers to fast
forward through television commercials, advertising
budgets were fat. For Frankie this meant Cristal
champagne, convertibles, grilled steaks, swimming pools,

fashion models in bikinis and the like. Frankie was the unofficial social director on that production, it seemed, as he would invite various characters encountered during the production to join them on these evenings. The first two nights hosted an Elvis impersonator who owned a wrought iron balcony location on Dumaine Street used in the commercial, and Buck and Elwood, the gay couple who were the owners of a wooden balcony location they had painted pink. On the last day in the city, before heading out to the swamps of the Blood River near Lake Pontchartrain, the production would be blocking traffic on Rampart Street and the New Orleans film commission assigned a police officer to control the flow of traffic. The policeman on set wore a Canadian Mountie styled ten-gallon campaign hat, and a gray uniform buttoned up tight as a drum, replete with sidearm. Frankie walks over and introduces himself.

"Hey man, how ya doin'? I'm Frankie." He extends his hand and they shake.

"Charlie," he says. The cop looks him over.

Frankie refers to a few of the beautiful models posing on the second floor wrought iron balcony. "Having fun?" Frankie comments.

The policeman glances up for a second. "Deys awright," he says in his New Orleans accent, seemingly unimpressed.

Frankie smiles. He's not buying it for a moment. They're gorgeous and Frankie knows the cop knows it too. "You know, we work hard during the day and all, but in the evenings we throw a little party back at the hotel," Frankie says, examining the cop's face. The cop is listening, but he's not exactly jumping for joy. "You'd be more than welcome to join us," Frankie adds, seeing potential for something special. The policeman folds his arms on his chest.

"Party?" the cop comments in a doubtful tone.

"Yeah," Frankie says, smiling at the thought.

"You a Yankee, ain't ya?" he asks, his tone approaching disdain.

"Yeah... New York City."

The policeman regards Frankie with a doubtful expression. "Ain't no Yankee know how to party!" the cop states, as a matter of fact.

Frankie is more than amused by the policeman's unexpected impassioned response, however he will not be challenged for his ability to party! Least of all from a policeman! Not even one from the Big Easy...

"I wouldn't be too sure about that, Chaz," Frankie says with a smirk. Policeman Charlie gives him a doubtful look. "Really... you should drop by... We have expensive champagne, ice cold beer, boiled crawfish, we'll be grilling up some steaks..." Frankie continues... Charlie remains unimpressed. "And ummm... you see these lovely ladies?" Frankie adds, referring to the models having a few laughs on the balcony, "They'll slip into tiny bikinis and jump in the pool for a swim... It's a good time. I promise," he says enthusiastically, with information he feels should be the clincher.

Charlie the cop looks up towards the balcony, considers the offer for a moment then says, "I guess maybe I'll come by for a beer."

The crew wraps the shoot and the inner circle heads back to the Casa de Marigny. Frankie puts on some music, the production assistants fire up the grill, and a few of the models jump in the pool...in their tiny bikinis.

Still in full uniform, Charlie the cop shows up. Frankie brings him a cold beer. They stand by the side of the pool like sore thumbs, sipping beer and listening to New Orleans R&B.

The cop turns to Frankie and asks, "You got any papers?" Frankie has a quizzical look on his face, unsure what the cop means. Charlie the cop pulls out a lid sized bag of marijuana from inside of his uniform shirt.

Frankie smiles impressed, imagining how Charlie the cop may have confiscated the bag of weed. "Uhm... no, but I know where I can get some... hold on a second," Frankie skips over to the production assistants and soon returns with some rolling papers, and rolls up a big fat joint.

He and Charlie the cop light up. The attractive make-up artist, Kim, walking by smells the marijuana. She stands there a moment, looks at Frankie and Charlie the cop in full uniform and somewhat astonished says, "You're ...smoking grass with our policeman?"

Frankie looks at her and smiles. "Yeah, want a hit?" He passes her the joint.

Hesitantly, maybe a bit nervously, she takes a puff. Seeing that Kim is unsure what to do next, Charlie the cop holds out his hand to her. She passes him the joint.

"Kim, Officer Charles. Charlie, this is the lovely Kim." Frankie says, smiling at the wonderfully strange introduction.

"Hello, young lady," Charlie the cop says to her, with a big smile.

"Hi," says Kim giggling a bit. Frankie loves it.

The exchange is even better than he had hoped would happen when he invited Charlie the cop to join them. "Look, you guys, I have to take care of something important. I'll back in a bit." Frankie says. He smiles at the both of them, hoping they won't mind if he leaves them alone together. Kim is still giggling as Charlie puffs on the joint, so Frankie scoots off.

Frankie had promised his friend Lil' Queenie that he'd meet her at 'Jimmy's' to see a friend of hers perform, and didn't want to miss it. He's glad he is able to put Charlie the Cop and Kim together so he could skip off and catch the show.

He returns to the Casa du Marigny around midnight to

find the place quiet with the exception of a few people in the hot tub at the far end of the pool. He walks over to find Billy, the gay wardrobe stylist, Kim the make-up artist, one of the models and Officer Charlie in the hot tub naked, two ice buckets full of beer at their side. Frankie looks down at the scene with a huge grin on his face.

"I see you decided to stick around," he says, smiling at Charlie the Cop.

"Yeah, …toined out not so bad afta all," Charlie says, smiling as he cracks open a beer with his handcuffs.

"Who are you?" asks Billy, speaking to Charlie the cop. "I've been in this hot tub with you all night and I have no idea who you are."

Kim the make-up artist rolls her eyes at Billy and says, "Billy, Charlie's the police officer who was on the shoot with us all day."

Billy's eyes light up. "Oh really?" he says surprised. "I've never been in a hot tub naked with an officer of the law before."

Without missing a beat Charlie looks at Billy and says, "That's ok son, I ain't never been in one naked with no faggot before."

§§§§§

Seated at the bar in 'Girls! Girls! Girls!' Frankie chuckles at the memory. He decides to go over and introduce himself to the Police Officer, hoping he knows Charlie.

"Sure... I know Charlie," the policeman says smiling.

Frankie tells him the story about the hot tub.

The policeman laughs and says. "Sounds like Charlie, all right. Hehehe..." He looks at Frankie. "He told me about that night. Braggin' how he made it with a sexy make-up girl from New York in a hot tub," he says, guzzling his beer. "I'll be damned. All this time, I thought it was a tall tale. Hehehee. Son of a bitch was tellin' it straight." He looks at his watch. "Gotta go, son." They shake hands. "Nice talkin' with ya, friend," says the cop.

Frankie smiles, "You too, pal." The policeman walks toward the exit... "Hey, officer," Frankie calls out. The policeman turns to face him. "Give Charlie my best!"

"Will do, pardner," answers the policeman. He watches the cop tip his hat to Mama Terry and make his exit. Frankie sits at the bar with a fond smile, happy he was able to give Charlie some cred.

§§§§§

Once again Frankie is alone. He's given up on Chip and figures the Midge is enjoying his educational experience at the Bangkok Spa and Body Rub, not to have to worry about him. And Dan had given up the quest hours ago, preferring a more personal quest, Frankie imagines. He sits down at the bar next to a young raven-haired stripper. Although she has toned muscles, wears black spandex bicycle shorts with cowboy boots and a tight black bustier, her dark almond shaped eyes and high cheekbones give her an exotic Middle Eastern look.

"I was fifteen when I became a vampire," she tells Frankie.

Even now, long past those early teen years, she snaps on a piece of chewing gum as she speaks. Pulling it out of her mouth and stuffing it back in repeatedly. Her huge ruby red lips in contrast to her pale white skin seemed to match Frankie's vision of a vampire, or vampiress, I guess you'd have to call her...

"They took me into this cold wet basement in the Quarter," she says, sipping her cocktail.

"Candles were burning everywhere. I remember that I recognized a few of the people," she continues, snapping her gum.

"They didn't seem to know me, or if they did, they sure didn't show it. I was scared shit!" she laughs.

She takes a long hard drag of her cigarette, continuing her story through a cloud of exhaled cigarette smoke.

"They performed this whole long ritual, chanting and shit. They all seemed to be really into it very deeply. It just made me tired. Finally my friend took my hand and gave it to this tall, kinda older woman, Moira," she sighs when she says 'Moira'.

"Moira held my hand tight and walked me to the middle

of the room."

Frankie watches her intently. She gazes out into space as she speaks, chewing her gum, occasionally looking Frankie directly in the eyes. She possesses a quality that is actually somewhat refined, in spite of her style of speaking and her mannerisms, which were both obviously learned here, at the bar...

"She had this really long black hair and wore this skin-tight long black gown, she was very beautiful," she says, looking Frankie in the eyes and smiling.

"We stood there face to face and she began to kinda stroke my cheek with the back of her hand. Her fingers were so cool... I felt embarrassed because everyone was watching us. She looked deeply into my eyes, then smiled," she says, remembering the moment fondly.

"Then she pulled my face even closer. I could feel her breathing on me. I shivered 'cause I felt her teeth on my neck. It didn't hurt or nothin', but I remember thinking I would fall down if her arms weren't tight around my waist. Then she just sucked blood from my neck. I'll never forget how it felt."

She pulls the gum from her mouth in a long string then puts it back in. Her eyes look up into Frankie's, smiling.

"Then she made me suck blood from her leg, down here," she shows Frankie a scar on the calf of her leg, where he imagines she has since initiated others in this same way. He bends down under the bar to see the scar up close. It sure looks like a scar made from teeth. Frankie feels her hand on his head, very gently.

"I was kneeling on the cold floor of the basement. She ran her hand along my head like this, as I sucked the blood from her," she continued. "Then I began to purr like a cat, and soon my whole body was convulsing."

Frankie raises his head. She looks at him and smiles. Lighting a cigarette, she continues through a puff of smoke.

"I've been on a steady diet of human blood for over a year now," she says.

Frankie stares at the raven haired stripper with a certain degree of incredulity. Then she appears, floating into the bar from the back room. A young Drew Barrymore as the Angel of Death the way Michelle Pfeiffer might play her, in a Veronica Lake hairdo; sultry, lithe, fragile... Frankie is completely taken by her. The image of her creates an immediate passionate longing in him. The young vampiress can't help but to notice Frankie's sudden interest.

Without hesitation, he asks, "Who is that? I want to meet her."

The Angel of Death notices his interest and glances over her shoulder to look his way.

"She's my lover," says the Vampiress, with a smug look on her face.

She spins on the barstool and throws the Angel of Death a kiss.

"Is she a vampire too?" Frankie asks.

Frankie hasn't diverted his gaze, from the moment the Angel of Death entered from the back room. She stares at Frankie with a coy little smile. "What a face!" he says.

Not one guy in the bar approaches her. They're too afraid to. As well they should be. They can't figure her out. She's very different than the other girls here. Other strippers work the room, trying to get customers to buy them a six-dollar glass of cheap champagne at the bar, in between their dance routines. The Angel simply sits there at the bar alone, slowly puffing away at a cigarette through her long sleek black cigarette holder.

Frankie can't believe his eyes. He gazes at her admiringly and thinks 'Here's a gorgeous woman rich in character. A true individual being herself, come what may. In society at large, and especially in the 'Girls! Girls! Girls!' strip joint, she is an anomaly. A walking talking strip teasing anomaly,' Frankie tells himself, sipping his whiskey through his sudden chuckling grin.

"What's so funny?" asks the Vampiress.

"Look at her," Frankie says. "Most people are afraid to show their differences from everyone else. Believing that the more they're like everyone else, the less their imperfections will be noticed. Most of us end up deciding it's not worth the effort to be as perfect as we can be, just for the privilege of being ourselves. It's easier just to be like everyone else," he says. "Of course, if everyone did that, then who would we be?" Frankie says, smiling at the Vampiress.

"Wow! That's such an interesting way to look at it" says the Vampiress. "I knew you were a cool guy."

Frankie can see that the Angel of Death's behavior probably costs her money she would otherwise make in tips. Perhaps she simply doesn't care. It's her part in the scheme of things at Mama Terry's strip joint. And she fills the bill perfectly.

Even though this is a strip club and customers can get any of the strippers to speak with them by simply buying them a drink, all the guys shy away from the Angel. They can't seem to get a handle on her. Perhaps, they think she's a little strange. Frankie loves everything about her. He loves illusions and here's one he won't have to work at. It's ready-made, just waiting for him to jump in.

It was always a treat for Frankie to find something to interest him outside of New York City. The long stretches in between the decadence of the inner cities in America scared the shit out of him. All those trees and the endless rows of corn... It was a fear that had allowed him to develop sort of a boozer's radar. Give Frankie a local bar to hide in and he was fine... and he could always find a bar, wherever he was. In his travels he learned that there are bars tucked away in the most unlikely remote areas all across the country. He has managed, at one time or another, to find a bar near abandoned oil wells, deceased industrial areas and on the outskirts of fringe locales of nearly every kind. He even found a bar in the middle of a cornfield once. Ah, paradise! He shot pool with a potato farmer and took sixty bucks off of him.

Boozer's radar aside, Frankie feels out of place whenever he leaves New York City. He can't help feeling that he sticks out like a sore thumb whenever he leaves the inner city environment. He can sense that he's different from everyone else, and that they all see it too. He stepped into a small town bar in farmland Wisconsin once and a drunken unkempt woman seated at the bar took one look at him and said, "You ain't from 'round here, are ya?"

In New York City during the 1980's homeless people were everywhere and nobody seemed to care, as long as you didn't end up in someone's building when you didn't belong there. The thing about New York City, though, is that most people are trying to be unique and different because they want to look cool. Unfortunately they end up being just like someone else trying to be unique and different in their feeble attempts to look cool. So they become part of a club, a genre …just another demographic. If we were to simply follow our hearts and believe in who we really are, it wouldn't matter if we were different, how different we were or how many other people were like us. We would be ourselves and realize all the treasures inherently in us that nobody else has. Wouldn't that be a major achievement and discovery?

That is true cool.

The Angel is unique, as different as they come. Different enough for Frankie to believe she's the real thing. And perhaps she is, but this isn't the dynamic that will allow him to find out. Not really... Nonetheless Frankie is looking for a detour and he's convinced this is it. He wonders how much money he has left. Maybe he can catch the Midge on the way out of the Bangkok Spa and Body Rub. He suddenly has to have both of these girls! That always takes money or a lot of luck. Neither of which Frankie ever seems to have enough of. He wonders what time it is and checks his watch. He has a full day's drive coming up with the crew. He doesn't want to have to suffer through it overly exhausted.

You see, at the moment Frankie doesn't seem to have the good sense to stop and think. He's letting lust rule his every move. While this is happening, Baby Doll, the girl he truly loves, is back in New York. Only she won't love him back. This is his balancing act, his way of retribution. This experience is his ode to freedom. His personal freedom, which may now be properly named Hell. There is only one place to go from here. The world of no worlds... the abyss... the dark secret night through which all is forsaken and little revealed... a magical place where time ceases to exist... a netherworld of titillating fantasy. In other words, a hotel room with two hot young women, both strippers, one of whom claims to be a vampire... a hungry vampire!

§§§§§

Time and Money... it seems we are always at the beck and call of these cruel partners in the march of mankind.

Time holds the secrets to all the events of the world, big and small, personal and impersonal. What wouldn't be significantly if not drastically different but for Father Time himself? The mere fact that he will pass us only once, ...painfully in some instances, eerily benign in others.

Money. Money is a truly evil invention. Money binds us to activities we would otherwise have little or nothing to do with, activities which prevent us from being ourselves.

Time and Money: This combination is the toxic avenger of mankind. Thwarting us in the noble quest for our lost essence!

§§§§§

Frankie's only concern right now, however, is how to make time stand still. If he can figure out a way to be alone with these two lovers it would, if only for a little while...

Baby Doll has several wildly promiscuous female friends who often feel the urge to enjoy wild orgies. Thanks to Baby Doll, Frankie is fair game. He's had the opportunity to experience several ménages-a-trois. He's discovered that the degree of secret unspoken dialogue between two women is mysterious and immeasurable in this situation. As a man, there were moments when he feels himself to be a complete outsider. Frankie took notes his first time with two women in bed. The notes didn't help him the second time... He thinks that maybe this time he'll finally figure it out.

He is sinking to the depths. Not only of his own character, but sinking to the depths of human life itself. Frankie is falling deeper and deeper each moment he sits with the Angel at the bar. Her face... the little twist she gives it. She is a master of illusion, a natural actress. Her intelligence is enormous. Not that of physics or mathematics. No, it is the intelligence she possesses in her entire body. Her command of the world of illusion she has set forth before him. The one Frankie can not wait to plunge deeper into. It is a wonderful and fascinating place. You see, where she has brought Frankie and where he has allowed himself to go, there is no time. They have, for the moment, beaten Father Time at his very own game.

The flip side will wait, and happily. Because the longer it does, the more immense it becomes, until it looms large as Everest. And when it crashes down on him, he'll know it, because it hurts so badly. Down it comes, an avalanche of sin, and the time he thought had stood still has just passed him by. Only now there's an expensive price tag attached, with only one form of payment due: his very soul.

After about an hour or so at the bar with the Angel of Death, Frankie agrees, following his base instincts, to join her for a short run in the back room. In many ways, he knows what's there before he arrives. Not the details, of course... no, the details of any experience are unique to that particular experience. It's part of the illusion. It's what captivates our interest. Makes us choose linguine over fish or roast beef, red over black or white, beach over mountain, whiskey over bourbon or vodka, blond over brunette or redhead... We live for variations of the same thing. But, were it not for this streak of childish optimism in all of us, we would wither away and die instead of waking up each morning. Some like to refer to it as selective memory or self-deception. Frankie chooses to call it living. After all, each of us, without exception, is subject to the impulsive instincts inherited with life itself. There is a price for living that we each must pay. It is our primary motivation, our instinct... to gather for comfort. In the modern age, due to our technological capabilities combined with rampant mental illness, expressions of these deviated instincts are multiplied times pi.

§§§§§

It is amazing what the working class will accept as a good time. Frankie is offered a small table behind a dusty swamp curtain near the entrance to the men's room. He buys a mandatory expensive bottle of cheap champagne and the chance to get to know his Angel a little better. Which roughly translates into 'she sits on his lap and gives him a hand job'. Naturally every swinging dick going to take a piss in the nearby men's room attempts a quick peek. Even as dark as it is, Frankie can see her unique beauty, holds in the close-up. She is extremely soft and tender. The Angel understands what her job is and accepts it. It is her choice and Frankie knows it, yet there is a part of him that feels responsible for her, a part of him that will have to be suppressed if he is to enjoy this experience at all. Yes, and she'll help him to do that. She understands how to avoid the inherent sadness of the situation. Certainly the booze doesn't hurt on that account. He keeps waiting for her to lean over and bite his neck, but it never happens.

VI

A Man Thing

"In only six months a man can learn all that there is to know of
bullfighting. For some men in this time they are now ready to face the bull.
Some are ready in one year or two, others become ready in five years.
Some men, however, are never ready to face the bull."
Hernon Orndazza, matador – Mexico 1989

Frankie's back in New York still terrified of losing Baby Doll. Plagued by the thought, he sits alone at his computer sipping whiskey, writing an ode about her. *She is an old wise man in the body of a beautiful young woman,* he writes. *I can't stop thinking about her.* He taps furiously at the keyboard for a while, then writes... *If you are a publisher you're probably scanning your desk for something else to read. If not, you're probably turning on the TV or reaching for the phone.*

The truth is that right now Frankie's burden of existence, aside from paying the rent, is learning how to live, not write. All of his life he has been chasing something unknown to him. Only now are inklings of it beginning to peek through mysterious shadow, even though they have existed for a long, long time.

Like many of his peers on this seemingly wretched planet, Frankie has spent decades unable to see very much good anywhere. Only greed, anger, lust, avarice, hate, pride and envy. He harbors a misanthropic notion of 'So what?' 'Up yours, you fascist pricks!'. What is it that is really wrong, though? Deep down? He doesn't know... He has a distinct feeling that maybe he never will. Perhaps it's simply a matter of taking life into his hands come what may ...manning the ship, as it were. It's about being Gary Cooper in a hurricane of shit. Being John Glenn in the lunar module, alone... Yeah, it's about balls! Courage!!!

Frankie wants to be strong! Strong as... John Wayne. Yes! He wonders if John Wayne would have liked Cherry Garcia? 'Who am I kidding?' Frankie thinks to himself. 'He would have eaten it by the gallon!'

He thinks back to the first time he met Baby Doll. He was on a music video shoot he had written the concept for. They were on location up in Harlem, and there were so many attractive women on set he barely notices her. Only a few months later, he would be completely enraptured by her. She was a good friend of the rock star the music video was being shot for. If she had known then what Frankie's life was like the day they met, she would never have returned his calls.

Frankie lives on East 12th Street in the East Village. A neighborhood the NY Post calls Alphabet City. A few doors down from Frankie's apartment sits the Newcomers Motorcycle Club. The Newcomers are a sloppy bunch who take back seat to the Hells Angels, and are comprised primarily of jail guards from Rikers Island. Some of them claim to be ex-cops, but most of them are prison guards and Con-Ed workers. Somehow they're able to install 'Motorcycle Parking Only' signs on the street corner out front and hassle anyone who parks in their spots. Their club is a long dark corner bar that was once a Steamfitters Pub. No longer a part of the NYC landscape, these were pubs that opened at 5 am to accommodate the all-night schedules of NYC steamfitters.

Frankie drives a 1973 Buick Riviera he affectionately calls the Tucker. One hot summer day, his buddy Tim and he exited a cool dark movie theater in Murray Hill, stepped into the hot Sunday afternoon sun having just seen the Coppola film 'Tucker: The Man and His Dream', walked up to the illegally parked Riviera and decided that it was now the Tucker.

Finding a legal parking spot in NYC is not a simple matter. And as the 'Motorcycles Only' parking spots are often the only ones available, Frankie parks the Tucker in them all the time ...windows wide open, beer cans half full, joints in the ashtray, coming home shit-faced at five or six in the morning. The Newcomers don't seem to mind. If it were an Audi with a ski rack or something they would likely have bounced it down the street. But, as it is a bright yellow 1973 Buick Riviera Frankie never locks and calls the Tucker, they drink beer on it, roll over it like overgrown kids and make out with their girlfriends on the hood. Frankie doesn't mind one bit. He thinks it looks good with a few bikers stretched out on it spitting into the wind.

Then, there are the works salesmen across the street. They only sell works. Frankie can't really figure out why they don't sell the smack to go with it? They sit across the street from his apartment against the fence of the defunct park with the decrepit basketball hoops in it, on milk crates or half-broken chairs salvaged from the Catholic school up the block, listening to the Mets game on the radio, drinking beer, getting sloppy and selling works. One of them, Boots, pimps whores out of his baby blue Cadillac with a Local Motion sticker on the rear window. They are the raunchiest hookers in town, too. Boots often tries to get Frankie to take one home. Luckily Frankie is never quite desperate enough. Besides, he's much too proud. Boots and company address Frankie as the Big Man. And they even watch his car. Many a day finds Frankie waking up from a three-day bender to find the Tucker half up on the curb with the windows wide open. Boots would be listening to the afternoon game, selling works and drinking beer with Bernard and Sidney. Imagine that... Sidney! A little wiry black guy from Alabama named Sidney. Bernard spots Frankie and dashes across the street, running circles around him, as he makes his way to the Tucker.

"Yo Big Man, some dudes tried to clip your hubcaps and your radio and shit, but I tol' em; dat's the Big Man's car. He's cool, ya gotta leave it alone man. He'll bust your ass up! Yo, Big Man, you got three dollars? ...And the headlights was left on too... and the left blinker was blinkin' like crazy, man! ...Just three dollars? Surely a big man like you can afford three dollars..."

Naturally he can ...what could he say?

For the life of him, Frankie can't figure out why these guys treat him with such reverence. Sure, Frankie often brings a six-pack as a gift for Boots, Bernard and Sidney when he goes to the bodega for supplies. And of course the three dollars are mounting up. Not that they always get it! No way! Often times, Frankie doesn't have three dollars. No, it's something else. A reason Frankie has no knowledge of ...or at least no present memory of. He can't fathom why these illegal drug paraphernalia selling street thugs hold him in such high regard. If they only knew how wary he was of the neighborhood, the thieves, the bikers, the crack heads, and heroin addicts, they probably wouldn't treat him with such a deep respect.

One day Bernard mentions something that cues him in. Frankie is sitting on the hood of his car, having just bought a few cold ones, listening to the ball game with Boots and Bernard for a bit before meeting up with his buddy Tim, when Bernard says it.

"Yeah... Big Man, you a bad mothafucka. That punk ain't never comin' back to this neighborhood. No sirree!"

A fragmented memory flashes through Frankie's mind, but then disappears just as quickly. He suspects that, in a blackout, he had kicked the shit out of someone and they all saw it. Naturally, he can't ask anyone. But it's a clue, a clue to a part of himself that he fears and worships at the same time.

It's possible that Frankie is an inspiration for them. Here's a guy obviously living on the edge, in a way one of them... but he's rockin' and rollin' too. He has his own apartment, he usually has a couple of bucks to spare for beer... he has cool clothes to wear... a hot ride. From their point of view, Frankie is just a really cool guy making it work. They admired him.

§§§§§

When Frankie was sixteen, he was beaten up by a greaser from his neighborhood every time he ventured into Tom's Corner, a local bar, to drink twenty-five cent beers and hustle pool. Chicky Zilner's face is forever etched in his brain. In fact, Chicky beat Frankie up every time he saw him, no matter where he was. Frankie could be walking down the street minding his own business, unaware that Chicky is cruising by in a car with some friends, when the car would screech to a stop. Chicky would leap out of the car, chase young Frankie down and beat the living crap out of him right there in the street while his friends sat in the car howling with laughter. Frankie still couldn't tell you exactly who Chicky Zilner really was, or how or where they first met, or even where he was from, but he loved him. Frankie thought Chicky was the coolest guy he'd ever known. Eventually Chicky took Frankie under his wing and taught him self-defense in the form of karate. The relentless beatings were the set-up and test ...to see if Frankie was a worthy apprentice, apparently. During this phase, when he'd see Frankie walking down the street, he would still chase the young Frankie down and attack him mercilessly. Only now Frankie was expected to counter attack, which he did. However the price was that the beatings are far worse than they were before. Frankie never knew which bar Chicky would show up in or what block he'd be driving down.

Frankie would be minding his own business, sipping a beer at the bar when, without warning, he's being dragged across the floor by the scruff of his neck, out to the street to be beaten up. Or, he'd be strolling down the sidewalk on his way to meet some friends and wham! Kick to the head, elbow to the gut, headlock, flip, punch to the face.

By the end of that summer, Frankie got pretty good at defending himself. One night he flipped Chicky onto his back and stun-punched him right in the face. Frankie was so shocked by the act, and became so frightened by it, that he ran all the way home through backyards, leaping over fences, swinging from trees and scuttling under bushes, too afraid to look back. Frankie didn't go anywhere unless it was absolutely necessary for weeks after that. As it turns out, that was the last time he would ever see Chicky. Now, all these years later, Frankie can't help but wonder what Chicky might have thought at that moment. Frankie grins as he imagines Chicky with a big smile on his face that night, rubbing his jaw and nodding in approval, as he watched Frankie run away.

§§§§§

Ever since he was a frightened schoolboy, Frankie has been challenged to fight. Back then, by rowdy classmates, since then, by practically everybody else. He always tries to wiggle out of it somehow, shaking in his boots from the darkness and sheer beastlike idiocy of nonsensical violence. Eventually, though, he's pushed too far. At which point he will pummel whoever is messing with him into the bleachers, or the fence, or the parked car, or the desks, or the lockers, or the juke box, depending on which incident he were to recount. Frankie just doesn't understand how to use violence as a means to an end. Maybe because he's never believed that violence can be used successfully as a means to an end in the first place ...unless it's absolutely necessary for self-defense.

§§§§§

Frankie was twenty-one years old the first time he traveled to Mexico. He and his girlfriend, Mandee, ended up in the little town of San Miguel de Allende. Actually, it wasn't that small by Mexican standards. With few exceptions, such as Monterrey, once you leave Mexico City, it's mainly small towns anyway. San Miguel de Allende was a gorgeous spot with a few thousand people, twenty percent of whom were Europeans and American ex-pats, called 'pensionados' by the locals. Who for one reason or another, needed the buffer of a foreign border, or their currency stretched out to the peso, which the peso gratefully provided.

The legendary matador, José Ortega Cano, is in town,

and Frankie is anxious to attend his first bullfight. The town buzzed with excitement. Mandee and he had met and were now traveling with a couple from California, Bill and Inga. Bill was a cameraman in Hollywood, and Inga was California girl hippie mama beautiful.

Bullfights traditionally take place in the afternoon. Because of this, there are basically two types of tickets, the shady side and the sunny side. Affluent Mexicans, judges, royalty, clergy, politicians, wealthy Americans and Europeans occupy the shady side. In sharp contrast, the sunny side, being far less expensive, is filled with the working poor, town peasants, young people and whoever else managed to get up the eighty-five pesos to get in. Being young, adventurous and, along with Frankie's relentless urging, they opted for the sunny side, agreeing it would be more exciting. It was absolute anarchy.

The stands were already packed when they finally found a spot for all of them to sit together. Frankie's girlfriend, Mandee, sat to his right, Bill and Inga to her right. Two cantankerous young Mexican men sat to Frankie's left. There were seven bullfights scheduled for that day.

Once the festive and colorful traditional pageantry of music and dancing, ending with the parade of dignitaries in the ring below, are over, the fights begin. The two young Mexican men seated to Frankie's left offer him sips of the cheap warm beer they're drinking. Frankie politely refuses. They are relentless and by the third bullfight it has became uncomfortable. The two young men were drunk, rowdy and absolutely insistent that Frankie accept their less than appealing offer of warm flat shit beer. Frankie was forced to refuse ...repeatedly.

The two men didn't have any roses, the traditional item one normally throws into a bullring as a token of congratulation or gratitude for the victorious matador, so had thrown much of their clothing into the ring instead. Being as impassioned as they are toward the fights, they have long since sent in their shoes and hats. Each time they did so, they would howl and yell loudly, then twirl the objects over their head, before finally bestowing them upon the victorious matador. Frankie watched as the less than gracious gifts flopped into the bullring below alongside roses, Cuban cigars, ladies' panties and the like.

The whole thing comes to a head when the one nearest Frankie begins twirling his dank smelly tee shirt over his head, screaming praise for the matador who had most recently killed his bull. It hits Frankie in the face. The guy was obviously loaded, so Frankie decides that he was just being a jerk and didn't realize what he had done.

A few moments later the tee shirt hit him in the face a second time. Frankie got the attention of his girlfriend, Mandee, Bill and Inga.

"Did you see that?" he asks, less than happy. None of them had seen it. "It's happened twice already!" Frankie exclaims. "We're talkin' a sweaty dank smelly tee shirt, too!"

"Calm down, Frankie. I'm sure it was just an accident,"

Mandee insists, trying to comfort Frankie, who was already at wits' end.

"Hey look, they're just a little loaded," adds Bill, pointing at the drunken Mexican guys with his chin.

The men continue to cheer loudly. "They just love the fights," adds Inga.

As irked as he was, Frankie calms himself down and focuses on the fights below. He keeps an eye on the drunk Mexican's tee shirt, just in case. This time he saw it coming and ducks to avoid being hit by the sweat soaked odiferous tee shirt. Only, as he did, so did the tee shirt. It hits him square in the face. The third time was one too many. Frankie grabs the tee shirt and pulls the guy in. Now they're face to face, screaming expletives at each other. Neither having a very impressive command of the other's language, it's more of a spitting contest. Things are about to explode when a group of rough and ready men in the immediate vicinity stand up. Despite the intense ferocity of his exchange with the drunken Mexican man, Frankie senses their presence and looks at the rows behind him to discover ten murderous faces staring him down. Bill sees it too. He is frantically whispering for Frankie to sit down. He turns towards Bill, "No way! Fuck this guy!" Frankie rages. Bill remains seated, scared shitless. Mandee and Inga are so frightened they dare not even look. Who can blame them? Never having let go of the tee shirt, Frankie turns back to the young drunk Mexican man and stares him down angrily, holding on tight to his half of the tee shirt.

Frankie knows what this is about. It's happened all his life. The young Mexican man is screwing with him to see what he will do. This is his turf. All his friends are there, and Frankie is the lone gringo. The murderous faces haven't moved an inch and appear more than ready to pounce at any moment. It doesn't matter. Frankie has reached the boiling point. It's a standoff: a Mexican standoff, to be exact.

Bill continues to plead with Frankie, screaming under his breath, "Are you crazy, Frankie? You'll get us all killed!" he warns, as does his girlfriend, and Inga.

"Frankie please! Just sit down! Those men are dangerous!!" Mandee begs.

"Frankie!!!" Inga whisper shouts… "Please!"

"Frankie, just sit down and forget it," Mandee screams as loudly as she can under her breath.

Frankie can't do it. The drunken young Mexican man and Frankie each hold on to their piece of the tee shirt, tugging at their respective ends, face-to-face and fist-to-fist. The bullfights continue in the arena below, but halfway up the sunny side of the stands finds Frankie and the young Mexican mano y mano, fists raised, screaming unkind obscenities at each other. They may be screaming in a language the other doesn't understand, but the message is loud and clear. Neither of them is backing down. The murderous looking men remain standing, doing their best to intimidate Frankie. They sneer at him while making threatening sounding comments to one another in Spanish. It seems they're brewing something up. An attack feels imminent. Mandee is near tears, shaking like a leaf. Inga is hiding in Bill's chest, his arms wrapped tightly around her. The three of them huddle together awaiting catastrophe. The situation appears hopeless. That things are about to explode seems inevitable, when an old Mexican man, his long white head of hair with a beard to match, seated on the top row, begins to laugh. It starts slowly, but then evolves into Walter Huston's howling laughter in 'The Treasure of the Sierra Madre', knee slapping and everything. All the murderous faces turn to look at the old Walter Huston character. He's having a good old time watching the scene, and laughing it up. It was very contagious laughter, and before long one of the murderous faces joins in ...then another and another. Soon they're all in uproarious laughter. The raucous Mexican man with the tee shirt and Frankie begin to laugh. Frankie lets go of his half of the tee shirt and they hug a manly hug. It was a test and Frankie had passed. They just wanted to know if he was willing to stand up and fight for himself. No pussies on the sunny side, please! Frankie reaches into his bag and pulls out a bottle of Herradura. Frankie never went anywhere in Mexico without a quart of tequila. He raises it high into the air. The previously murderous faces cheer. He pulls the top off and takes a long healthy swig, figuring he will likely never see it again. Then, with a great gesture of newfound friendship, Frankie passes the bottle to his one-time adversary, the young cantankerous Mexican man with the dank tee shirt. He gulps some tequila and passes it up to the closest murderous face. As the Bullfights continue below, Frankie watches every one of the murderous men drink until the bottle reaches the old man. He raises the bottle to Frankie. Frankie takes a bow, a big smile on his face. The old white-haired man takes a healthy swig. More cheers. A couple of bullfights later, the bottle finds Frankie again. He guzzles some, insisting that Mandee, Bill and Inga each have a substantial gulp or two also, and passes it on.

§§§§§

One would think that Frankie might begin to string these experiences together, but he can't do it. The thought of violence is just too repulsive to him. It doesn't occur to him that lifestyle can indeed add to or detract from the possibility of violent confrontation. To this day, deep down, he feels himself to be a chicken shit. He is fundamentally afraid of violence. It disturbs his psyche. He is against it as a solution to almost anything. It makes him feel like a big dumb idiot having proven he is courageous, strong as a bull and tough as nails over and over again, yet reaping little or no actual benefits from the experience of any of his violent confrontations. Can it be that now, after all these years, at the age of thirty he is finally figuring it out?

The clincher comes when a production assistant, Michael Boise, drives him home from the music video location up in Harlem the day he met Baby Doll. He'd been smoking marijuana and doing coke for most of a hot July day. His head was buzzing. They have the director's car; a 1970 black Cadillac convertible, and, along with them, a gorgeous model featured in the video, who Boise was to also drive home. She asks to use the bathroom, so Frankie invites them up. They smoke a joint and have a few drinks. At one point, while Boise is in the head, Frankie and the beautiful model begin to slow dance to some jazz music Frankie had put on. They share a long wet kiss. She is wasted and so is he. Frankie considers asking Boise to leave so he can be alone with her, but decides against it. As much as he would like her to stay, he is totally exhausted. And they have one more day of shooting, an early one at that. Frankie tells them that he needs rest and they leave.

The director's classic convertible has a few hubcaps missing and, being the young foolish kid from LA he is, Boise decides it would impress the young model and make his boss happy if he were to clip two off of Boots' Cadillac parked across the street from Frankie's apartment. Boots catches him red-handed and pulls a gun on him. Boots, Bernard and Sidney attempt to force Boise into the back seat of Boots' Cadillac. Somehow, Boise gets away and manages to buzz Frankie's apartment. The fact that the buzzer for a building on East 12th Street and Avenue B in 1987 works properly is a significant stroke of luck for Boise, to be sure.

All Frankie knows is that his buzzer is ringing off the wall only moments after they left his apartment. His head is already reaping the benefits of a soft pillow. He gets up reluctantly, walks to the intercom pushes talk and says, "Yeah?" then pushes the listen switch. Through the speaker he hears, "Frankie man! These guys are gonna kill me man!! I need help down here!!!" He can tell that Boise is in deep shit, or at least that he is scared to death. Either way, he has to help.

He takes the flight of stairs down to the street to find Boots, Bernard, Sidney and a crazy dope dealer who hangs out with them every once in a while, when he isn't in jail. Frankie always forgets his name, even though he holds onto his birth certificate and some of his legal papers in the apartment somewhere for safekeeping, as a favor, since he'd been living on the street.

They have smashed the windshield of the director's Cadillac, and have poor Boise by the throat.

"Let him go!" Frankie screams.

"Yo, Big Man, this here's a friend a yours? Yo, Big Man we didn't know," Bernard yelps.

Sidney chimes in, "Yeah, Big Man, we didn't believe him but, yo, Big Man he tried to clip Boots' caps man, check it out."

Boots looks at Frankie apologetically with a shrug of the shoulders. The crazy dope dealer still has the tire iron in his hand.

"Frank man, I didn't know these guys were your friends... I just wanted to get Ben these hubcaps ...he's been buggin' me for months, man, to find hubcaps for the Caddy!" Boise cries.

Frankie looks at Boise, then at the car, then at Boots, Bernard, Sidney and the crazy dope dealer. They all stand there in the middle of the street. He turns to Boise. Suddenly Frankie is in charge! How the fuck this happened he can't fathom. These tough, homeless street thugs, drug dealers, pimps and insane asylum attendees are apologizing to him for scaring his friend, smashing up the car and getting him out of bed because Boise had stolen their hubcaps. Frankie is touched. He feels somehow vindicated, powerful and maybe a little silly. He takes Boise by the hair. He's still shaking, scared half to death. Frankie wonders, 'Why aren't I?'

"You stole Boots' hubcaps?" asks Frankie, taking Boise by his shirt. "What the fuck is the matter with you?" he screams. "These are my friends!" he yells, then smacks Boise in the back of his head.

"I'm sorry, Reno..."

"Say you're sorry to Boots."

Whimpering, he says, "I'm sorry, Boots."

"Louder!"

"I'm sorry..."

"All right," says Boots, "All right..."

"Yo, fuck that. Lets smash this muthafucka up!" the

crazy dope dealer screams, holding the tire iron high up in the air near the director's Cadillac. He's still very pissed off. Frankie tries to remember his name... 'What is his name? Eddie. Yeah... Eddie. No, Freddie!'

Meanwhile, the bikers on the corner at the Newcomers Motorcycle Club are getting a kick out of the whole thing. Wondering if the car would get smashed... if heads would roll... would blood be shed? So was Frankie....

Then the cops show up. Frankie turns around and there they are. Quietly seated in their cruiser in the middle of the street, inches behind him. It occurs to Frankie that the young model is gone. 'Where did she go? Is she okay?'

"What's going on here?" the cop asks Frankie.

'What is going on here?' Frankie asks himself. 'They're asking me! Why me!?! What the fuck is going on here? What am I... the fucking mayor or something?'

Freddie drops the tire iron out of sight. They're all looking at Frankie. Bernard, Boots, Sidney, Freddie ...Boise. Frankie looks at them one by one, silently looking at him. Then, at the cops who sit there waiting for an answer. Frankie knows they won't wait all night.

"Oh, nothin'," Frankie says.

"All right then, you wanna get out of the street?" says the cop.

Frankie saunters to his side of the street, noticing just then that he's barefoot. His shirt is buttoned up three buttons wrong. Forget his hair and bloodshot eyes. The cops look him over then drive away.

"Get outta here, Boise," says Frankie.

Boise wastes no time jumping in the director's Cadillac and speeding off, probably still shaking.

A few days later, Frankie walks over to the Tucker, which is parked in front of the Newcomers Motorcycle Club. Willie, one of the bikers he would talk to occasionally, is there, sitting on an old bar chair in front of the club with his feet up on a milk crate.

"Hey, Willie" Willie nods his head. Frankie walks over to him. "Were you here the other night?" Frankie asks.

Frankie has to know what Willie thinks of the way he handled the hubcap situation that night. Somehow he feels as though Willie would know. Frankie was still unsure. He felt uneasy. Shouldn't there have been a fight? Retribution? "Give me those hubcaps you fuck, I'll tear your fucking head off! And fuck you! Now that you busted up the windshield I'm gonna fuck you up and take the other two caps as spares!" Shit like that...

Willie doesn't need to be told who he is. It's obvious. He's Willie, biker, a member of the Newcomers Motorcycle Club and a self-made philosopher.

He takes a sip of beer and looks Frankie in the eye. "There's no such thing as an atheist in a fox hole," he says cryptically.

Gazing into the hot midday sun, Frankie thinks, 'Probably not, not a sane one anyway. A very clever trap, fear... how easily it leads to faith.'

Willie sits there on that old beat-up bar chair, his feet up on the milk crate... covered in tattoos, leather and grease ...and guzzles some beer.

"Yeah, when I first heard that I thought, 'bullshit!', but in the end ya gotta believe in the unknown," he looks up at Frankie, "That's where you get your balls!"

Willie slowly drinks back the rest of his beer and belches. "It's a man thing," he says finally. Then, without looking, he nonchalantly tosses the bottle over his shoulder into the dark interior of the old pub.

Frankie waits to hear the sound of the beer bottle crash onto the floor inside. Instead, the bottle ends up in the hands of Willie's' girlfriend, Louise.

Until Willie threw the beer bottle over his shoulder into the bar, Frankie didn't even notice she was there. The interior of the bar is very dark in contrast to the bright midday sun. Frankie has to squint his eyes to see her standing there. Her leather hot pants and cut-off see-through halter top do nothing to distract from the sheer lack of intelligence her body carries. Her face says it all; I'm a dim-witted broad. Her slightly bowed legs are covered in leather chaps, which come up to her chunky thighs. She's all tits and ass with a dumb face. It's the kind of face you'd only suffer through if you loved the person who owned it.

"Hey Louise, get me another beer, will ya?"

She stands in the doorway behind Willie, motionless, the empty beer bottle still in her hand, staring at the back of his head.

"Oh ...nice catch," Willie adds.

Louise smiles, turns around, and walks over to the bar.

Willie winks. "I found her in Jersey at the shore. She was puking behind a tree. At first I fucked her because she was so drunk, but then the next day... I dunno."

Louise returns with a cold beer for Willie.

"Thanks, baby." She stands behind him with her hands on Willie's shoulders... he licks her hand. Louise's eyes roll back into her head a little. Then she looks down at Willie admiringly. She raises her head and glances at Frankie with an expression that says, 'look what I got'!

"You want a beer?" she asks.

"Sure," Frankie mutters.

She disappears into the dark bar. Willie continues between sips of his beer. "I guess you can never figure love. It sneaks up on you." He looks up at Frankie. "Remember that," he states with authority.

Louise reappears and throws a cold beer to Frankie from inside the dark bar. He has to react quickly, but he catches it with one hand.

"Nice catch," Louise laughs, and then returns to her position behind Willie. Frankie opens the beer and takes a long swig.

Just then, a wiry little Latino teenager from the neighborhood comes running around the corner in a panic, flying a leather jacket in one hand, followed by a scream.

"Hey, get that fuck!"

Willie sizes up the situation quickly and dives on the kid with the jacket. He squirms beneath Willie's grasp. The man who just screamed catches up, out of breath. He bends over, grabs the jacket and rears back his foot like he's going to kick the kid in the gut.

"You scumbag!" he snorts.

"Fuck you!" the kid screams.

Willie grabs the man's boot just as it's about to make contact with the kid's midsection.

"Hey, cool it!" says Willie. "Grab the jacket," he says to Frankie.

Frankie does so without thinking. The guy is not happy about this, but bides his time. He is a frail junkie. He isn't about to fuck with Willie and Frankie. Not straight up, anyhow. Frankie keeps him in the corner of his eye. Willie takes the kid by his shoulders, and spins him face up.

"What the fuck, are you fuckin' Wyatt Earp or somethin'?" the kid yells, still breathing heavily.

Willie looks up at the junkie ...he's still gasping for air and coughing ...then at the kid, his head on the sidewalk, panting.

"You!" Willie says to the junkie. "Get fucked."

The junkie is confused.

"What do you mean? That's my jacket!" he yelps.

Willie looks at him. A simple authoritative statement from Willie follows.

"Blow me."

The junkie knows he's beat. He doesn't quite know how it happened, but he was through running after his jacket. He stands there staring at Willie in disbelief. Willie stares back. He's about to say something but then thinks better of it. He creeps away kicking the sidewalk, cussing under his breath.

"Get up, kid," Willie says, taking the jacket from Frankie. The kid gets to his feet. Willie stares him down for a moment, looks over at Louise in the doorway, then at Frankie. He hands the kid the leather jacket.

"Get outta here," Willie snorts.

The kid splits, managing to get the jacket on as he runs off, glancing back shaking his head.

Willie sits back down slowly ...easily. He glances over as the kid moves up the block with his new leather jacket.

"See what I mean?" he says looking up at Frankie, "It's a man thing."

VII

Man or Mouse

"...Ashes to ashes and dust to dust, if God won't have him the Devil must."
English Burial Service (1711)

Frankie is doing his best to keep his life from careening into the abyss. Not only with Baby Doll, but the whole mess ...which is to say, he is keeping the cat well fed. His impulse is to tell practically everyone he knows to go to hell. They are all fucking with him ...people he works with in the film business, his friends, parents, siblings, but especially Baby Doll. 'To hell with them all!' he tells himself.

He often thinks back to the night on the street with Boise and Boots' hubcaps and the things Willie said. He didn't think he could ever truly ascribe to Willie's definition of what it means to be a man. Screw him too!

It's just proud anger, though. It's like, 'Hey, go screw yourself, asshole... oh... by the way, how's my hair?'

Long before Frankie got into the film business, he helped to manage an SRO Hotel on East 25th Street in Murray Hill. SRO stands for Single Room Occupancy and that's just what it was ...the loneliest place in the world. Filled with drunks, drug addicts, pimps, hookers, transvestites, transvestite hookers, the old and deranged. These are truly forgotten people. Forgotten, despondent and unloved.

One such resident was an old drunk named Charley Berg. Charley got fall-down drunk every day. He was a large man who'd worked his entire life as a carpenter, so was fiercely strong ...for an old drunk. Until a decade or so before, the Carpenters' Union was right across the street from the hotel. Never married, it appears that Charley walked across the street one day, got a room and never left. By the time Frankie arrived there, Charley was just a dirty old sot who would terrorize the entire neighborhood with his drunken behavior. The first time they met, Charley violently attacked Frankie with his cane for no apparent reason.

"You dirty Jew kike son-of-a-bitch!!! You're a Jew! A Jew!!!" Charley screamed angrily at the top of his lungs as he swung his heavy wooden cane at Frankie, wheezing and coughing from the effort. For some reason, after getting to know Charley, Frankie loved him nonetheless.

As much as Charley enjoyed terrorizing the entire neighborhood, he especially enjoyed the daily badgering of his decrepit neighbor, ex-burlesque dancer, Catherine Smythe. Catherine hadn't left the confines of her room, and the shared bathroom at the end of the hall, for twenty years. Her clothing old and raggedy, she didn't own a television and her radio rarely worked. To be truthful, the radio worked fine. One day Frankie asked her about it. She turned the knob to prove it didn't work. He checked behind the dresser and saw that it was unplugged. Frankie plugged it in and it worked perfectly. He found a station of old show tunes. She seemed really happy and even danced for a few moments. A few days later it wasn't working again. Frankie would plug it in again and the next time he'd go by it wouldn't be working, so he'd plug it back in. After a dozen or so of these exchanges, he gave up.

Because of this strange problem, her only contact with the outside world was Charley ...and the New York Post. He'd go out shopping daily for her supplies; Lipton tea, milk, a sandwich and the Post.

He'd hand Catherine her groceries, take a seat on the decrepit old chair, sip his cheap wine, look at her then begin yelling obscenities. "You're a whore!" he'd often start...

It fascinated Frankie the way Charley pronounced the word 'whore'. It rhymed with 'sewer' the way Charley said it. 'Who-er!'

Catherine usually left her door opened wide. Frankie supposed it was because she needed the occasional human contact with the outside world. Leaving your door open in a trashy SRO hotel will provide little of that, but it was all she had. In the four years Frankie worked there, she walked down the stairs to the lobby only once. She wore a dated yet dressy women's overcoat, a green Easter bonnet and house slippers. Frankie almost didn't recognize her. She thought she was having a heart attack. Frankie called an ambulance, and the paramedics said she was fine. When they left, she just went back up to her room.

Her room had one window, an army cot style bed, a wooden chair and a beaten up dresser. The walls were painted a faint green ...maybe thirty years earlier. Charley would take a seat on the only chair in the small eight by ten foot room berating Catherine, who sat directly opposite him on the bed. This routine was a daily ritual for them.

As uniquely bizarre these exchanges were, they seemed affectionate toward one another. No matter what Charley said, Catherine never once raised her voice, became angry or insulted. One day Frankie decided to sneak up and hide in the hallway near her room to watch the scene he'd only previously heard from the hotel office or the lobby every day since beginning the job a month earlier.

"You're a who-er..." Charley would begin, "...and your motha was a who-er too. I knew your motha you stinkin' old who-er... Scum o dee oight! An' your sistas was all who-ers too! You was all a bunch a who-ers!!!" he'd growl at the top of his lungs.

"Oh, Charley..."

Catherine was a deranged version of Edith from 'All in the Family'.

"...My family was good to everyone! Mrs. Cranski downstairs, when she couldn't feed her kids, my mother would buy her groceries. We were good to the whole neighborhood... Charley," she'd say, her speaking and mannerisms polite and demure, bordering on insanity.

"Yeah... you was good to da whole neighborhood alright... spreadin' your legs for 'em, dat's what. You old who-er... You're a who-er!!!

He enjoyed sitting on parked cars, sipping wine while shouting insults at women walking down the sidewalk.

Frankie would often find Charley out on the street near the hotel, screaming and waving his cane at some unsuspecting passerby. Or at a family in their car, hurriedly rolling up the windows scared out of their wits because dad had beeped his horn at him for leaning on the car to take a sip of wine, and Charley was now going for dad's head with his cane.

One day while walking to work, Frankie spotted him seated on a parked car a few doors down from the hotel, blazing drunk on some Wild Irish Rose. Frankie stopped to say hello at the same moment an unsuspecting attractive young couple are happily walking by holding hands ...enjoying a beautiful day.

"Sell it!" Charley screams.

"Sell it... you who-er," pointing his cane at her crotch.

Shocked by the comment, they scuttle away as quickly as they can, frightened at what might've happened next.

"Who-er!!! You're all who-ers!" Charley continued, pointing his cane at other women strolling by...

As strong as Charley was, he would often become so drunk that, when he fell down, he couldn't get himself back up again. The bathroom he used was down the hallway, a few rooms away, so there was always something to deal with.

One night while working the swing shift, a young couple from Berlin who had an S&M routine playing at Show World came to the desk and said that there was a naked man lying in the hallway, screaming mad. Frankie knew it had to be Charley. He decided he better go check it out. Frankie could hear him yelling and screaming as he ascended the stairs to the third floor.

"Hey, get me up damn it!! Hey!!! Catherine you who-er. Get somebody, damn it. You stinkin' old who-er!"

Charley banged his cane against the wall and door making a racket. Few in the place dared go near him. If the Germans didn't happen to be leaving from the same floor, he might have stayed like that for hours. Finally he sees Frankie.

"Hey you, get me up, damnit!" he screams.

"Charley, ...what happened?"

"Who's that? Frankie?"

Frankie leans over him ...all two hundred and fifty pounds of him, lying buck naked in front of his door, hanging on to his cane, unable to get up.

"Yeah, it's me, Charley," Frankie says reassuringly.

"Hey Frankie" he says suddenly, calm and friendly-like. "I left my key inside," he mutters, out of breath.

"Okay, just gimme a minute... I'll go get the key," says a compassionate Frankie.

"Alright," he says like a big helpless baby. Frankie rushed, got the passkey and ran back up the stairs. It wasn't easy, but he finally got Charley into his room and up onto his bed.

"Now get outta here, you piece a shit!" Charlie screams, waving his cane around like a wild man. "Get out, damn it!" he yells, nearly zonking Frankie in the head.

Frankie was so astonished at Charley's reaction that he couldn't move. He stands there in the doorway, frozen, staring at Charley, who continues wildly swinging his cane trying to bash Frankie in the head. But Frankie's a little too far away and kaboom, down Charley goes.

"Aw shit! Help me up, damnit!" he yelps.

"My God, Charley. C'mon already," Frankie pleads.

Frankie gets him back up on his bed.

"Gimme my cane," he pleads.

Frankie hands Charley his cane. Charley takes the cane, holds it high in the air like he's going to start swinging it again and screams, "Now get outta here, you punk, and stay out!"

Frankie walked away, dumbfounded, shaking his head in amazement.

Could it be, all these years later, it's that same lethal mix of pride and anger at the root of all Frankie's problems? What is it that he's so afraid of? He is afraid of losing Baby Doll. Afraid he won't measure up in his chosen profession. Afraid no one will love him. Afraid he isn't good enough and that none of his dreams will come true. Afraid he'll never be respected by his peers, because he's a fraud, and that they are all going find out and hate him because of it.

'So what?' Frankie decides. 'Fuck 'em!' He garners dislike for people he hasn't even met yet. And he's too afraid to ask why. To sit there all alone in a dark room and figure it out. It's easier to run. To find any detour to any place other than the one he's in. It'd feel like being crucified on the cross for Frankie to just sit there and take it, but he's running out of people to blame. Despite that, he continues to believe the world always does him wrong. He figures Baby Doll is God's way of saying, 'Here, take this at least. It's the best I can do for you right now…'.

It's easy to pretend to his friends that Baby Doll is a good thing. Even if few of those who ever get to meet her understand why he is in love with her. 'Fuck them too!" What he knows is simple enough. Frankie sees it as a trade off. It isn't easy getting great looking women into bed. Even if he gets a high degree of nonsense along with it, he has one who loves him. One who desperately wants him to fuck her like an animal every moment they're together. A woman who invites other great looking women home with them to have wild sex parties in her penthouse apartment. 'Whoa! Hold on just a minute! What's going on here?' Frankie thinks in absolute astonishment 'I can't even pay my rent, yet I have my own harem!'

Yet, no matter what he does or how he does it, he never quite feels like a man. Not in the full sense of the word. He can't shake the feeling of being just a frightened little boy or worse, a mouse being pursued by the big angry cat. Everything he does is in direct response to what the beastly cat does. When it's asleep, he will roam around freely and attempt to satisfy his needs, wants and desires, often with great bravado, describing to the other mice what he's going to do if he ever gets his hands on that fucking cat. Or tell them about all the cheese he's going get. They'll be sorry all right! Cause he's going keep all the cheese for himself and they'll all have to kiss his ass to get some, even that fucking cat! But as soon as the cat stirs, Frankie runs for cover. The cat takes on many forms. Girls, jobs, cops, traffic, parents, siblings, bosses, truck drivers, the keyboard of a computer, you name it!

VIII

Turning a Buck

"You are served 'Duck Soup,' nothing more. But you can hardly swallow
this broth; it is a turbid liquid in which bits of wild duck and guts
imperfectly cleaned are swimming...it is far from tasty."
Anton Chekhov, "Across Siberia"

Frankie is an American, it is late in the 20th Century and he lives in New York City. He is free, white and, well ...thirty-one. It seems unlikely that he will do something simply because it is worthwhile. Even if he knows deep in his heart that it's the right thing to do. No, the act must be generating cash profits either for himself or for someone else ...so they can purchase everything money can buy! Amplified to some degree by Madison Ave, the entire modern world operates on this premise, and it feels inescapable to him.

There was a time in his distant past, when the idealism of youth reigned, Frankie would make the necessary sacrifices required to do something simply because it was worthwhile, but at the time this story is taking place he wants it all, and not getting it is driving him crazy.

He is so close to everything that he wants, he can taste it. So close, yet so far... He wants money! He wants power! He wants beautiful women and more money and more power. Expensive sports cars, yachts, mansions, and drugs, lots of drugs! More money. And a private masseuse! In this unlikely fantasy there is a mansion filled with gorgeous women of every race, color and creed ready to fulfill his every command. 'Yes Frankie-san', they would giggle, as they scuttled about pleasing him, caring for him, obeying him... loving him! His mind spins out of control at the thought of it! 'Yes!' his mind reels. 'Give it to me! Give it all to me!' He feels he absolutely deserves it. He knows he does! He just can't figure out how to get it. And nothing can convince him that it requires patience and the willingness to start at the bottom and work for it. He wants it now!

He turns on the television and flips through the channels hopelessly, his mind churning. 'I want that... I want that... I want that... I need her... I want that... I would try that... look at that! ...I definitely need her... Oh my, look at that! Oh!!! Oh!!! Oh my!!!! People actually live like that!!! Oh man... I have to get some...'

And in the face of these morbid fantasies, he fails to see the irony of his complaint that people aren't satisfied with the simple pleasures anymore. That everyone is selfish, corrupt and dishonest.

Frankie is the only person he can think of to come out of the 1980's poorer than when the decade began. He feels as though everyone he knows is making money: Big money! And those who aren't are just losers, misfits and malcontents. He remembers learning how many of his friends and business associates had voted for Reagan and still love him. It's 1988 and they're still raking in the cash. Frankie wonders if he were making truckloads of money, would he feel the same way? He was twenty-eight years old when he realized he had never voted. Frankie figured that the wrong person was going to win anyway, because they are all the wrong person. He feels that with rare exception politicians have long abandoned the high ideals set forth in the Constitution. That ethics and service to the people have been traded in for self-serving profiteering. And they are all in the same corrupt system, so what can it possibly matter?

Frankie can't take sides. Life is all gray area. He finds that he can agree with points of view from practically every stance he considers, because they all reside in partial truths in order to sell themselves to their constituents. Is it the risk of choosing sides, or the fear of breaking a few eggs? Where does he draw the line? He can't decide.

§§§§§

It's ten am at The Crossroads bar. Frankie is the only patron in the place. He's seated at the bar, writing in his notebook and speaking with his favorite bartender, James.

"It's a rat race!" James insists.

Frankie looks at James and smiles.

"Ah yes, the old adage still rings true! The ever-popular rat race... I have a few words here about that," Frankie says, between sips of whiskey. He refers to the pages in front of him and reads:

"Each day we all come face to face with the decision to either join the sacred rat race or plunge to the depths of obscurity and poverty."

"...and failure," adds James.

"Failure... I know it well. And not only in the world around us, but in our own minds."

James listens intently. Frankie scribbles some notes, and finishes his straight whiskey. James pours him another. He takes a sip and reads from his notes.

"We inhabitants of this, the free world, in one form or another, must worship at the well-lit altar of fame and fortune, so that one day we too may arrive at celebrity heaven ...or at least be able to afford similar distractions," Frankie retorts.

He rolls a cigarette.

"That's what life has become ...one big distraction. 'Get me outta here' is the anthem of modern man," he states, lighting his cigarette. "Attempts to accomplish this ambition are achieved at any cost to our selves or anyone else ...on a myriad of levels."

"Get me outta here!" James says with a big smile. "...the 1980's in a nutshell."

Frankie laughs. "It'll likely get worse before it gets better... And because of this dire need, we must find ways to escape our ill-fated lives. The act of growing up has been relegated to the ability to lie, cheat and steal. It costs money to get outta here, after all..." says Frankie, stopping to relight his cigarette.

"I gotta tell ya, Frankie, it's a good thing you write this stuff down," James remarks.

"All the time. I'm not sure it's any good, but I have reams of this stuff," he says. He turns the page, looks down and reads.

"There is a point in everyone's life when they must decide the moral argument: honest and poor, or criminal and rich. Only the crime here may apply mostly to crimes against one's self. Not living by the simple adage, 'To thine own self be true', might possibly be the greatest crime we can commit, 'cause it leads to all the others."

"To thine own self be true..." James repeats, deep in thought. "To the bard!" he adds, raising a glass.

"To the bard," Frankie clinks James' glass and shoots one down.

"Naturally, one's ability to advance by one's successes and failures often mirrors the time in each individual's life that this crucial decision occurs. The quicker the better; moderation is a sin here!" Frankie announces. "There's a saying about that... ...sleeping when we're dead..." he looks at James hoping for an answer.

"They'll be plenty of time to sleep once you're dead..." James says, with resolve.

"Ah... the nuance of poetry in prose..." His eyes perk up.

"Wait! That's it!" he says excitedly.

"What's it?" James asks.

"The Horror Continent!" Frankie answers.

"The horror what?" James inquires, unsure of what Frankie is talking about.

"Remember that old one-eyed junkie I told you about? Herman?" Frankie asks excitedly.

James thinks for a moment... "Yeah... yeah... that crazy old eccentric guy who lived in that funky hotel you ran."

"That's him... Herman... he was something else," Frankie says fondly. "He told me an amazing story one night about a place he called The Horror Continent. I think I just figured out what he was trying to say." Frankie lifts a nearly full glass of whiskey and takes a long drink.

"I'm not sure he even knew what it meant," Frankie suggests, deep in thought. "But, I think I get it now."

He looks at James with a big smile. "Funny how it came about."

James pulls up a stool behind the bar. They're still the only ones in the bar.

"Herman Cohen," Frankie says endearingly.

"Herman and I were neighbors on the D Floor of The Carlton Arms Hotel when I knew him," Frankie says, with a sweet affection. "I introduced him to my friends as

Uncle Coe. There's Edgar Allen Poe, then there's Uncle Coe!" he says with a big smile.

"The man was so off the charts, it just would have taken far too much explaining as to why else we hung out together..." Frankie says smiling. "But family... everybody can accept that. He was my neighbor on the D Floor when I lived there for a year or so. He had a very creative mind. All right-brain... just never had a chance to develop it for one reason or another..." he says rolling a cigarette.

"One day I'm in my room and I hear him moaning and groaning something terrible." He looks up at James, "I mean, I could hear him loud and clear from inside my room with the door closed. It sounded as though he was pleading with someone he was terrified of... 'No.... no... go away... I beg you... please...' Frankie says, mimicking Herman. So I go over there and knock on his door, see what's going on...."

James sips his drink...

Frankie continues... "'Who's there?' Herman asks frantically. 'It's me, Herman. It's Frankie.' 'Frankie? Is that you?' he asks... 'Yeah, Herman, it's me. Are you ok? What's goin' on in there?' " Frankie says, stopping to sip his whiskey.

"I figured he needed a fix, y'know?" he says, looking at James.

"So I say, 'Herman, look if you need some money...' 'No

Frankie! No!!! Go away! They'll get you!' I had no idea what he meant by that, but I could tell he was truly upset," he says, sipping his whiskey.

"I mean, the guy was not normal, by any means, but I had known him for close to a year when this happened, and as much as he did some pretty strange things during that time, I'd never seen or heard anything like this before." Frankie stands up and stretches for a moment.

"So I knock again and ask him to let me in. 'No Frankie, go away! It's for your own good... believe me! They'll get you Frankie. Once they see you it's all over. Once they recognize you, they'll never leave you alone. It's too dangerous! Now go! They're evil spirits. You have to trust me, for your own sake, go away.' I didn't know what was going on in there. But whatever it was, it had him totally spooked."

Frankie takes his bar stool and sips his whiskey, thinking back.

"He was actually very brilliant, despite his endless oddities. Herman would look through a newspaper and find points of view any writer would give his right arm to be able to see! Brilliant, really..." Frankie shakes his head in fond remembrance of his old pal.

"So now, I'm really worried, y'know? I mean, I loved the poor guy... I bang on the door again. 'C'mon Herman, let me in. Maybe I can help.' 'No Frankie... No!!!' " Frankie says, imitating Herman. He shakes his head, rolls his eyes and smiles.

"This goes on for some time. Now it's getting really spooky. How long can the guy hold out moaning and groaning like that? It's obvious he needs help. I have to figure out a way to convince him to let me in. I knew once I was in there I could calm him down."

"C'mon Herman, there's gotta be a way you can let me into your room. I'm sure I can help."

"This goes on for what seems like forever and then finally after pleading with him for what must've been twenty minutes, he says. 'Ok Frankie... ok, I have an idea!' he says, kind of excited. 'Look' he says, 'you find a disguise so they won't catch on to who you really are! Ya see? Then I'll at least feel secure enough for your safety so I can let you in. But find a good disguise cause if they see you... if they identify you, they'll never leave you alone. But! If you find a good disguise, you can fool them,' he says, sounding hopeful for the first time since the whole thing started," Frankie says, smiling.

James is fascinated.

"So I say, Ok, Herman, I'll be right back. 'Hurry Frankie! Hurry... I don't think I have much longer. Ohhhh!' He sounded like he was dying in there." Frankie sucks down some whisky.

"And the whole time he's moaning and groaning in agony. Mortal terror, right... 'Ohhhhh!!!' " he says, mimicking Herman again. "I mean these are really disturbing sounds... yelling and screaming... pleading..." Frankie imitates him, "No.... Please leave me alone....

Oh!!! Aghhhhh!!! Ohhhhh!!!"

"And by now I'm feeling a little queasy, but I have to help the guy. So I run back to my room, happy that he's finally gonna let me in ...right? Then it hits me... what the fuck kinda disguise am I gonna find? I go through everything! I try to make something out of the pillowcases. That didn't work. I tied socks together trying to make a mask but then I couldn't see through it so that was no good. I tried towels, bed sheets... even a baseball glove... nothing worked. Nothing I had was gonna disguise who I was. Meanwhile, Herman is sounding worse every second and I'm starting to freak out. Should I call for help? Y'know? What should I do? I gotta do something. He sounded like he was dying in there. Then a light bulb goes off in my head! I had just returned from Florida visiting my grandparents, and my grandma gave me one of those hairy coconuts carved into a head with painted faces on them. They still sell them in tourist shops all over Florida. Remember those things?" he asks, smiling for a moment.

"Yeah! Yeah..." James answers, nodding his head. "Ha! My aunt gave me one of those when I was a kid. Goofy looking thing!" he laughs...

"That's it!" Frankie says, smiling. "So, I grab this clunky hairy coconut head carving from the closet and go back to Herman's. I bang on his door hard. He sounds worse than ever." Frankie knocks on the wooden bar a few times.

"Herman! Herman! It's me, Frankie... I found a disguise! Open the door! Let me in! 'Is that you Frankie?' he asks... 'Yeah, it's me, Herman... It's Frankie.' 'Wait a minute, let me see,' he says, his voice still really shaky. He cracks open the door just enough to peek out. I'm holding the Coconut head in front of my face and he says 'Is that you Frankie?' 'Yeah, Herman, it's me...' I pull the coconut head away from my face so he can see it's me, right? And in a total panic he screams. 'No! Frankie no! Put it back! Put it back! Don't let them see your face! If they do your life will never be the same!' His entire body is trembling, right...'

Frankie says, a bit emotional from the memory.

James sips his whiskey. "Wow... unbelievable... I mean that's a crazy scene!"

"After some doing, he finally lets me in," Frankie continues.

"I grab a chair, sit down and do my best to calm him down, cause he's still a mess." Frankie sips his whiskey, thinking back a moment.

"I still figured it was possible that he just needed a fix. Maybe he was broke and too proud to ask me for a loan, so I offer him some money again, but that wasn't it. After a while of just sitting in his room talking, he calms down a bit. We're speaking about all kinds of stuff, when he looks at me with the most intense dire expression. He lights his cigarette and says, 'Frankie, have I ever told you about the Horror Continent?' I look at him, and he's very serious."

Frankie puffs his cigarette. "I say, no... What is it Herman? 'Now listen Frankie... this is very important,' he says, almost in tears.' "

James settles himself on the bar, listening intently.

Frankie continues... "He takes a long drag on his cigarette, looks me in the eyes and says.... 'While we're in our beds sleeping, ...innocently asleep, they come for us... stealthily in the night... when nobody's around. Then they torture us mercilessly all night long... They torture us until we are dead. And we wake up never knowing that we're actually dead. The Horror Continent.' He takes a long drag on his cigarette then puts it out in the ashtray. 'Remember what I said, Frankie. He looks up at me and just stares at me for a moment, making sure I'm listening. 'The Horror Continent,' he says. 'The Horror Continent,' and that was it."

Frankie and James sit there quietly for a moment.

"The Horror Continent," James repeats. "...Wow..."

IX

Jingle Bells

"The main reason Santa is so jolly is because he knows where all the bad girls live."
George Carlin

Frankie and Baby Doll have been together for nearly a year, seeing each other every chance they get. Frankie prefers her company to anyone or anything else. His family and friends rarely see him anymore. Forget putting in extra hours at the production office, if he happens to have one to put extra hours into. He is mostly unemployed around this time. In fact, Frankie is nearly always unemployed. Yet he never seems to have any time. Basically, though, avoiding the issue of employment for the moment, the distance between himself and everything else is growing wider at the expense of his extreme, passionate and desperate obsession with Baby Doll.

It's nearly Christmas and Frankie is experiencing high levels of anxiety wondering how he'll afford to buy a really wonderful impressive Christmas gift for her. He needs one that will compete with all the other wonderful gifts he's convinced she'll be receiving from God knows who. He just knows she'll be receiving sapphires, minks, paid invitations to Aspen, and all manner of expensive gifts from other men.

He's heard stories about the ex-boyfriends. At times their conversations about them seem endless to him. None of Frankie's friends understand the relationship. Not even Frankie and Baby Doll can figure out why they're together. One night while in bed talking, the subject comes up.

"If you're accustomed to a higher lifestyle than I can provide, what are you doing with me?" he asks in earnest.

"I don't know... I feel natural around you. You don't try to control or manipulate me," she says.

'Well, no shit!' Frankie feels like screaming. 'That's because I haven't any money! I'm lucky that I get to have sex with you, much less have you madly in love with me, to then try to control you as well!' He knows those words have to go through her mind just as they do his.

Experience is the name intelligent people give their mistakes. Sometimes pain is the more immediate. Frankie seeks experience but is discovering pain. His burden of choice is how to live each moment as though it is his last, without forsaking the past or the future. To die before he dies...

Death can teach us many things. Just as he did ole' Ebenezer Scrooge... It's the holiday season and all versions of Charles Dickens' "A Christmas Carol" are on TV. It's Death who finally catches Ebenezer's attention. The Ghost of Christmas Past couldn't do it. He tried to touch Ebenezer's soul by presenting his heritage and past experience. Ebenezer would have little of that as a true convincer. The Ghost of Christmas Present tried to do the same and wrap things up with a relatively mild review of the unseen in the present day. If Ebenezer wanted to see those things, he would have seen them a long time ago. The ghost of Christmas Future, he has a gig! He has Death in his pocket.

"Oh, please! Please tell me I'm not dead. I want to live!!!" pleads Ebenezer.

Sure, the ghosts of Christmas Past and Present rattled a few bones, shook things up a little. So what? We can go years drowning the feeling that we're wasting our life away and never change a thing. Just pour another drink, get another woman, another man, a new car, a new dress, you name it. Take your pick...

Sure, Frankie's not dead yet, but that's just the point. What he's done to waste, mutilate and otherwise attempt to fool Time, can sometime almost make him wish he were. Besides, he watched the version of A Christmas Carol starring Alastair Sim ...sober! It was just Frankie and Old Father Time and he wept like a child. You can fool some of the people all of the time and all of the people some of the time, but you can't pull one over on old Father Time. The world may well be a stage, and we mere mortals may well be the players, but Father Time and Mother Nature are the playwrights. And tragic-comedy is their forte.

Frankie is convinced that the best days the world had to offer are behind us. That no one does anything for love or adventure anymore. That our primary interests, in this day and age, are making money and gaining power. As much as Frankie despises it, this is the value system he feels forced to succumb to. As much as he disagrees with it, in principal, this is his vision of reality. That we make decisions based on personal gain motivated by fear. Fear of not being loved... Fear of not having as much as the other guy... Fear of him having more than you... Fear that you'll have to do things you don't want to do to get what you want, or even worse, just to survive. Fear that his penis is larger than yours. Fear that you'll look silly in front of everyone. Fear that everyone will hate you. Fear of everything that fucking moves. What is fear? Where does it come from? Who started it in the first place?

Frankie wondered... would he treat Baby Doll differently if he had lots of money? He couldn't answer the question with any degree of clarity. His imagination refused to provide the scenario that would allow him to create an accurate conclusion. As though such a situation was unthinkable to him ...having lots of money. Being broke isn't a dream of Frankie's, however doing things he finds loathsome in order to make money isn't any more of an ambition. And he hasn't figured out how to do what he wants to do and also make lots of money.

Because of this he is a failure.

People will do almost anything to make money, some more than others ...in varying degrees. To most of us, it is the most important thing in the world. Frankie is both disgusted and sympathetic to this phenomenon. Sure, he would love to have as much money as it would take for him to do whatever it is he wishes to do at any particular moment, without having to answer to anyone or anything. On the other hand, he's met people like this, too many of whom suffer from an exaggerated sense of entitlement. They forget that they're human beings. Authentic challenge has left them and they must resort to silly little games for amusement. Usually involving unsuspecting people's lives. It's sad, vulgar and revolting.

In any event, he didn't have any money... he never did! And, he probably never will.

Yet, he has to believe that it's possible, or he would never be able to get it up for Baby Doll. Especially since her take on their whole thing together is based on the idea that he will remain the same giving, loving, gentle man he is now, once he is rich and famous. And that they will live happily ever after screwing everyone they met, together...

That is her dream. Or at least that's how Frankie sees it. He often wonders how he has managed to buy into that one. Who would imagine that they are investing in the free love concept at the tail end of the 1980's. Her imaginings transcended polyamory... something just doesn't add up.

On the other hand, it makes perfect sense to him. Neither can remain monogamous, yet they each harbor serious jealousies at the other's infidelities. It's the only solution ...or so it seems. For Frankie, as long as he isn't expected to suck any cock, he was game for all the women she could bring around.

But just where do all these women come from? The question arose in his mind constantly. The answer came with Christmas, so did the cock.

§§§§§

"Daddy!" Baby Doll screams, as she jumps up and wraps her legs around him. He's just returned from a twenty-hour shoot in Coney Island stopping at home before heading to Baby Doll's to shower and shave. He's a bit exhausted but twirls her around and around. They kiss wildly, their groins pressed hard against one other. She tears his shirt off, then his jeans. She falls to her knees. Suddenly he is in her mouth, as she licks and sucks wildly.

'What's going on here?' Frankie thinks to himself. Mentally he hasn't quite joined in yet. 'I better get involved quick!' his mind tells him. It's as though he's watching the whole thing happen from far away. He feels like a voyeur in his own sex scene. The mirrors that cover most of her walls make it that much easier for him to mentally detach himself from the situation. It isn't long however before he rips off her clothes, lifts her up onto himself, holds on to her ass very tightly and fucks her violently while standing upright. She screams wildly at the top of her lungs. It seems as though he can't fuck her hard enough. They fall to the floor gasping for breath. After a while of just lying there, they begin to talk.

"You want something to drink?" she asks.

"You read my mind," says Frankie.

She gets up and goes to the kitchen, pours Frankie a straight whiskey and grabs herself a beer. Frankie gets comfortable on the huge pillows that are laid out on the floor near the fireplace. Baby Doll puts on some Miles Davis then sits down beside him.

They sip their drinks, enjoying Miles and the fire. She glances over at Frankie a bit nervous, suddenly. She fidgets for a moment, as her faint smile attempts to masquerade a grimace.

"You know what I do, don't you Frankie?" she asks, looking up into his eyes. He looks at her timid smile set perfectly between her sweet freckles, with a dumb look on his face, fearing his suspicions will become real and undo his pseudo-perfect world.

"What do you mean?" he answers, deep in his subconscious already knowing this is the beast he has been avoiding.

"You know," she says with a painful mixture of coy innocence and angst.

"I'm not sure what you're trying to say," he says, getting up to refill his empty glass.

"You know, Frankie... what I do for money, right?"

Frankie pours his drink and just stands there. Things are becoming tense and uncomfortable.

"You know I work as a call girl, right?" she states, her voice breaking a little.

As much as he had wondered... as often as the thought had entered the far reaches of his mind, he can't believe he is hearing it in words. From her!

He's crushed... mortified...

"You knew, didn't you?" she asks, coaxing him, her voice calling out for compassion, understanding and love.

He can't speak. If he is speaking, he doesn't know it. His mind is numb. He doesn't want to know. He wants no part of the power this little bit of information embodies to him. What would he do with it? He's too close now. 'Get me outta here!' his mind tells him.

"What about the trust fund? ...Your dad's life insurance money?" he asks, finally.

"That ran out, Frankie ...a long time ago," she says, looking down at the floor. "That's why I'm always so hard on you about money. I love you. Frankie, I don't want to do this anymore. I need someone to take care of me. I want to get married. I wish it can be you."

He's floored. What does he say? All he knows at this very moment is that he loves her more desperately than he has since he met her. He knows that he must save her, but he doesn't know how.

"I think you should go now," she says.

"I do too..." he says, finally ...sullen.

"I'll call you tomorrow," she says.

"Okay."

They hug and Frankie leaves.

X

Bad Day for a Flat

"Et tu, Brute...?"
Julius Caesar

Her door closes behind him. He presses the elevator button... It arrives... He steps into the elevator... It goes down... People get on... They're not real... It's like a dream sequence in an old German film noir. He walks towards Ninth Avenue, his mind in a dense fog trying to remember where he parked the Tucker. Crack dealers are everywhere. "Yo this and Yo that..." Things take on surreal proportions, as everything happens in slow motion. He just now realizes that there are a few inches of snow on the ground and that it is, at this very moment, snowing. He's walked six blocks without noticing the snow.

Finally he sees the Tucker parked a block away from her house. He's been walking in circles. He approaches the car, it's leaning to one side. He looks down. He has a flat. He opens the trunk, jacks up the car and mindlessly begins to remove the flat tire. It all happens apart from him. Frankie's there, but not really.

The tire gives him trouble and won't come off. The snow isn't helping. He's fighting visions of Baby Doll giving great head to one man after another. She's smiling up at them as they hand her hundred dollar bills. She is being showered with hundred dollar bills, falling like rain all around her. Many men's garish faces are laughing. Their laughter echoes in his mind. He shakes his head violently from side to side, attempting to dispel the unwelcomed visions.

Knowing how much she loves sex, he's convinced she enjoys every one of them. A thousand images race through his mind. It's not pretty. There are other feelings, mixed feelings. A person's shadow falls over him suddenly. He looks up. Standing on the curb near him is a drug dealer he's seen around her neighborhood. He looks down at Frankie crawling around in the gutter dealing with his flat tire situation, shaking his head from side to side in pity. Frankie can suddenly feel the snow on his face and his butt in the cold, wet gutter under the car trying to get the tire off. The sorrowful expression on the drug dealer's face gives Frankie an instant image of himself. The drug dealer just stands there puffing on a Newport, watching Frankie trying to wrestle the stubborn tire off.

"Bad day for a flat," he says cryptically. He takes a long puff of his cigarette, frowns and walks away in a cloud of cigarette smoke. If he only knew the truth...

Frankie begins to sob. Tears run down his face as he finally gets the tire off. He puts on the spare. Tears continue to flow as he tightens the last bolts, gets in the car and starts the huge engine. Tears are streaming down his cheeks as he puts it in gear. He moans and sobs as he drives the Tucker down Ninth Avenue. 'Bad day for a flat,' Frankie thinks to himself. He speaks it aloud. "Bad day for a flat," he has a giddy chuckle. "Bad day for a flat," he says, mimicking the drug dealer. He begins to laugh hysterically. "Bad day for a flat!" Frankie is completely bonkers now, laughing uncontrollably. He pulls over to the curb and tries to calm himself. He can't. He continues to laugh hysterically. He looks up and notices that he's in front of an old Irish drinking man's bar on Ninth Avenue. He sure as shit can't drive, and he can sure as shit use a drink.

"Bad day for a flat..." He can't stand it. Frankie is completely insane with laughter as he falls into the bar, tears rolling down his cheeks. His hands and face are covered in grease, and he's soaking wet from the snow that melted on him, mumbling and gurgling strange incoherent laughter. He sits down at the bar. The bartender walks over to him, a bit wary.

"What'll it be?" the bartender asks, eyeing Frankie watchfully.

Frankie looks up at him. "Harrrrhahahahaha harrrrohohohohhhh!!!!!" he says.

The sight of the bartender standing there wondering what in the fuck just walked into his bar has Frankie going even more then when he first arrived.

"Bad.... harharrrr hahahah ohoh ohhhohohoh..... Bad day...HA HA HA HA HA HA HA ho ho ho ho... wait ....No wait... Bad day for a.... HARRRRRRRRRRRRRRRR!!! HARRRRRRRRRRRRRRRRRRRRRR!!!! HA! HA! HA! HA! HAAAAAA!!!! HAAAAAAAAAAA AAAAAAAAAAAAARRRR!!!

Wait a minute ... Please Oh... Oh... Ohhh...... Please just a... Oh... It's just a... oh..........hold on.....Bad day for a flat!   HAAAAAAAAAAAAAARRRRRRRRRRRRRRRRRRR! HAAAARRRRRRRRRRR!!!   HA!   HA! HAAAAAAAAAAAAAAARRRRRRRR HA! HA! HA Ha ha ha ha oh oh ohh... I'm sorry... oh... I'm so sorry... Oh... ahem... Oh... just a second... oh... I'm sorry... aha... aha... oh... Uhm....I'll a... I'll have a, um... double whiskey straight up... please... ahem... I'm sorry... sorry... Bushmills. "

"A double Bushmills straight up then... Ok," he says briskly, with an Irish accent Frankie only now notices. The bartender walks down the bar and pours the drink.

Frankie looks up. Five people, all old drunks, a woman and four men, are looking at him like he's nuts and like they've seen it a hundred times before. They're all staring at Frankie, quiet and motionless. The bartender comes over and serves his drink.

"That'll be three fifty," he says.

"Yeah," Frankie answers.

He pulls out some money and places it on the bar. The five customers continue to stare at him with faces that ten-year old boys make the first time they light a firecracker, take three steps back and wait for it to explode. Frankie still feels really giddy. He sucks down the drink, then, looks up to find them all still staring at him. He looks back at them, afraid to speak a word.

Finally in a brogue accent, the man closest to him asks, "So... ya gonna tell us what the hell is so funny?"

XI

April Fools

"And though circuitous and obscure, the feet of Nemesis how sure!"
Sir William Watson, "Europe at the Play"

During the following weeks, Frankie discovers he loves Baby Doll more than he could have ever imagined. He has to save her! Rescue her from the horrible men who are sticking their penises inside of her. Every time he thinks of it he cries. She has related a bit of her family history, how she came to be a high priced call girl. At eighteen years of age in Malibu her mother introduced her to a man. He is the man she introduced to Frankie as her uncle. He's no uncle!

Why does he feel so sorry for her? Maybe it's the story she told him about her father committing suicide when she was five years old. Her father was a closet homosexual who held an executive position for a very conservative firm in the Northwest in the 1960's. He was found out, and became so distraught over it that he killed himself. But is any of it true? Frankie isn't a hundred percent sure about anything. All he knows is that he has to save her. A desperate need to be the Knight in Shining Armor arose in him like tail feathers of a peacock in spring.

If he could find a way to put enough dough together, he could rescue her, he thought. They could fly away to a

Caribbean Island, figure things out... get lost in the world. That's when he meets Egan. Egan is from Glasgow. He doesn't have a green card and so works an assortment of odd jobs to survive. He is a messenger, a shoe salesman, works in a hotel... and as a waiter. But what Egan really wants to do is to rob a bank. French thieves had recently pulled off an ingenious bank robbery in Paris by locking all the bank employees in the vault, then faking a live hostage situation. Negotiating for hostages as they were actually escaping through a tunnel they had prepared in advance, under the very street where a hundred French cops sat around waiting for the hostage negotiation to be resolved. By the time the cops figured it out, they were long gone. Those French thieves are their heroes. Frankie isn't sure what exactly is driving Egan to want to rob that bank, but as far as Frankie is concerned, if they can successfully rob a bank, he would finally be able to take care of Baby Doll. Egan and Frankie begin to explore the possibilities of actually robbing a bank. They spend many nights talking about it, trying to figure out which bank would work best. They decide a Midtown bank would cause the highest level of tension, hence the largest distraction, so will be the best option.

Then Egan scores an amazing job. He is hired as a bagman for mobsters who run a string of brothels on Second Avenue in Midtown. It's a one in a million situation that, for Egan, is nothing less than winning the Lotto. His job is to visit each brothel every four hours and collect the cash. He is given a limousine and an overweight lackey driver, and that's all he does. Collect cash from brothels! Oh there's a bit of accounting involved, as he must register the amounts in a ledger. At the end of the night he turns it into the office, a swank duplex in Midtown. For the life of him, Frankie can't figure out exactly how Egan got such an outlandish job. But it's a gem. They pay him well and he sure as hell doesn't need a green card. The pick-ups become larger as trust in him grows, and soon Egan is carting around as much as two hundred and fifty thousand dollars at a time. His conversation leans more and more towards how he could dump one night when he was loaded up with mobster cash.

Then one day Egan decides he has to do it. Frankie tries his best to talk him out of it. "This is the mob we're talking about! It's not the same as robbing a damn bank!" Frankie warns. In the end, Egan talks Frankie into helping instead. It isn't too difficult either, since all Frankie really wants is enough money to save Baby Doll. Now they need to figure out how to pull it off and get away with it. Other than mob retribution, the largest obstacle to successfully pulling it off is the driver. They need to take him out of play long enough for them to get away safely. Frankie and Egan brainstorm everything, from Frankie hiding in a nearby doorway and bashing the driver over the head with a baseball bat to Egan spiking his coffee. The driver is actually more like a watchdog and carries an old-school snubnose 38 revolver. A mean, growling simple-minded watchdog is what he is, too. His entire focus consists of keeping an eye on the money ...and on Egan.

Frankie is keenly aware that, if the driver catches him, he's likely a dead man, so whatever they come up with has to be sly, anonymous and very clever. Neither Frankie nor Egan are baseball bat over the head types and killing the guy isn't even joked about. For days, the two fledgling felons struggle with methods of distracting the driver long enough for them to get away with the loot. They entertain everything from a fake accident, explosions, and a fire, to a lady in distress and free donuts... It becomes apparent something more extreme is required, and that rendering the driver unconscious without actually hurting him is the only solution. But they're coming up dry. Then it hits him! Frankie remembers a story he had read as a child that occurs in the Amazon rainforest, where natives used poison dart blowguns as weapons. Egan will convince the driver to step out of the car while Frankie hides nearby with a blowgun loaded with a drugged dart. Frankie knows where he can get Ketamine, a fast acting animal tranquilizer known on the street as Special K. Sometimes called Super Acid, Ketamine is used recreationally by druggies, much like PCP, only its effect is instantaneous. The plan is for Egan to convince the driver that his tire is low, and when he gets out to check, Frankie, hiding nearby, will shoot the poisonous dart in the driver's ass with the blowgun. The second he's out cold, they take the money and run! The plan is simple enough, only it is reliant largely upon Frankie's ability to shoot a blowgun.

He gets his hands on one and practices for days. He becomes fairly proficient at dart blowing, and feels confident to go through with it.

It's the night they're going to rob the cash. There's a hard rain drowning the city. No drizzle... for once Frankie would welcome drizzle, too. Egan gives Frankie the address of the last pick-up for the night and Frankie is there waiting in the shadows of the doorway at the neighboring building when the limousine pulls up. Egan steps out of the limo and nervously glances over to where Frankie is supposed to be. Their eyes meet. Egan winks at Frankie, hidden in shadow wearing a long black raincoat to hide the blowgun ...a blowgun loaded with a poisonous dart and ready to shoot. Egan enters the building the brothel is in, smiling. A short while later Egan exits the building and rushes through the pouring rain into the back of the limo. Frankie does his best to keep his nerves in check as he waits for the driver to emerge. Finally the driver begrudgingly exits the car. Frankie checks the surrounding area to be sure no one is around. Egan watches eagerly from inside the limousine, holding on to the bag of money. The driver bends over to check the front tire, Frankie places the blowgun to his lips, aims and shoots. It's a great shot right into the driver's buttocks. His eyes roll into the back of his head and down he goes. Egan leaps out of the car with the bag of cash and they race around the corner to where Frankie had stashed the Tucker, laughing all the way. In large part from relief, to be sure, but also from the sheer thrill of having actually done it and gotten away. Plus, seeing the driver go down was just plain funny...

Within hours Egan boards a plane leaving the country out of JFK. Too pumped with adrenaline to sleep, Frankie stays awake all night reliving the high points of the theft. Two days later mob underlings come around asking questions. They had found a piece of paper with Frankie's address and phone number on it in Egan's apartment under the sofa cushion. Frankie could've killed him. But not even he knew where Egan had gone, and they couldn't prove anything. During the following weeks various gangsters appear to interrogate and threaten Frankie. They warn him never to tell anyone anything about the incident. They're worried it might give other bagmen ideas, plus it's an honor thing. They keep a close eye on Frankie for months. He never feels safe during this time. It isn't all that much money to them in the scheme of things, and it begins costing them more trouble than it's worth. Frankie knows they don't suspect him because he has a good alibi, but they thought maybe he could lead them to Egan. Eventually they just stop coming around.

§§§§§

Valentine's Day came and went, and March was coming to an end. Frankie grows more restless and desperate since the cat was let out of the bag on Baby Doll's extra-curricular activities. She does her best to make it worth his while, bringing more and more women around... they're crawling out of the woodwork! All coked up and ready to go. Frankie cannot be less interested. His heart isn't in it anymore, and he simply can't keep up with it all. Baby Doll, on the other hand, could have kept it going for years. She's younger than he is and it just doesn't occur to her that time is running out. Not even Frankie knows just how quickly.

Then it comes.

"I'm pregnant," she says, "and you're the father."

"What do you mean I'm the father?" asks Frankie, a bit astonished.

"I know it's yours, Frankie ...you're the only person I don't use a condom with."

He believes her. Neither of them is in the least bit prepared for this. He feels horrible that the child ...his child... is aborted. He knows he'll have to live with that for the rest of his life. Now there's nothing more to say. He weeps for weeks, even writes a song about her, and then it's over ...not a romantic feeling left.

Amazing, but that's how it happened. April Fool's Day, Frankie woke up and the pining was over. She continued to call him and it was hard saying no even though the feelings were gone, because the sex was out of this world... but the jig was up. He dug out what was left of his half of the Egan score and gave it to her. A short while later she called to tell him she was moving to Aspen. She was able to leave Frankie alone after that. It was probably for the best. As wonderful as she was, in his heart of hearts Frankie knows that he and Baby Doll weren't truly meant for each other after all.

Last Frankie heard of Egan, he was stuck in Egypt with a nasty case of Hepatitis B. They never did rob that bank, and Frankie was still broke.

XII

The Recurring Nightmare

*"...I remember, I guess I was about eighteen. I stood at the edge of a huge
swimming pool, Miami I think it was... ...the light shimmering on the water
...the hot sun beating down on my body... And I dove into that pool with
all the gusto, all the verve ...all the enthusiasm of a young man
about to conquer the world, his whole life in front of him.
The next thing I know, I'm sitting here talking to you. So live, because it
goes by (snaps his fingers) like that"*
Tony Curtis, Johnny Carson Show (1984)

Someone once told Frankie that insanity is doing things the same way over and over, expecting different results. At the time he didn't fully agree with that assessment. More likely he just wasn't ready to accept it. He went years not considering it as a measure for his actions. Remembered it though ...kept it in the back of his head... someday it was going to become valued information. That day was soon coming. He could sense it approaching as he traversed the razor's edge between two adages: 'Insanity is doing things the same way over and over, expecting different results' and 'If at first you don't succeed; try, try again'.

Frankie rarely made a cohesive plan regarding the direction his life was heading. Because of this, he never really knew what he was doing. He'd do it anyway, deciding that if it was a mistake, he'd know soon enough. If not, he would know that pretty soon also. Only, due to his excessive alcohol consumption, he couldn't remember what it was he did half the time anyway. His life was a mess. It became obvious things couldn't go on the way they were.

Frankie felt as though he were the last person in the world who was going to do anything about it. Not because he didn't want to. Only that he had no experience in creating change. Change was something that happened to him, not by him. Or so he thought...

§§§§§

Frankie was fifteen the first time he visited a strip bar. Barnacle Bill's up in Port Washington on the North Shore of Long Island. Barnacle Bill's featured an exotic dancer who was double-jointed. She could lick her own genitalia and did so every chance she got. It nearly ruined sex for him forever, seeing it. Yet each time she would do it, he was powerless not to watch. She'd get into position. Frankie would wince a little, peeking out of the corner of his eye. And then she'd do it. Men would howl. Dollar bills would leap onto the tiny stage behind the bar where she danced. It was awful, but Frankie was helpless to look away. He had to watch. He simply had to see this girl lick her genitalia. He rode his bicycle twenty miles just to see it. There were men there, and he was a boy. He didn't think he was a boy at the time, but he knows it now. He was just a boy.

By the time Frankie was sixteen he was a daily drinker and 'Barnacle Bill's' was only one of his hangouts. There was 'Tom's Corner' down near Roosevelt Racetrack. And

'The Shady Rest', an old-school roadhouse with Whitey the bartender that, on a Friday night in the 1970's, was full of underage kids drinking beer. Then there is 'The Evergreen'. 'The Evergreen' was the most remarkable among them. It was the kind of place where a person could truly lose track of time. It was always night inside the Evergreen. There are other bars that possess a similar quality, but the Evergreen was the epitome of them all. At 7:00 am the Evergreen was open for business. Frankie cut class a few times and went there. By noon he was buzzing like a hummingbird. He'd walk out into the hot midday sun, shocked to discover it wasn't midnight.

It didn't occur to him then that there was anything unusual about these forays into darkness. He was just a little ahead of his time. His mom had a different view of it, however, and one day she finally figured it out. Social Services had sent out mailers intended for parents, warning them of the signs to look for in drug and alcohol abusing teens. Frankie was playing basketball with his buddies on the dead end street he grew up on. He and his pals were drinking beer and snorting THC. At least they thought it was THC, it might have been PCP. Whatever it was, they loved it!

His mother walks over to the mailbox and finds the pamphlet. She reads it, right there at the mailbox. She immediately runs across the yard waving the pamphlet in the air... "Frankie, I know what's wrong with you, you're an alcoholic, you're an alcoholic!" she screams, arriving at the basketball hoop. "Mom, I'm playing b-ball here. Not now, hunh? Will ya...?" She looks at the ground, sullen, and walks away. He was too much for her by that age and she'd lost any influence over his wild lifestyle.

Suddenly it's twenty years later. He never did look at that pamphlet.

XIII

The Crossroads

"Mercy! Mercy! This is a devil...I will leave him, I have no long spoon."
Shakespeare: Stephano; The Tempest

Then something begins to happen. How or why it begins at this particular time is impossible to determine. It just comes upon him suddenly, yet, as though it was always meant to happen. The more he lets it happen, the more he realizes how much he has been preventing it from happening in the first place, and how close it has come to happening in the past. Also, how inevitable that it must now occur. Trying to prevent it, at this stage, would be like standing in front of a speeding locomotive expecting to not get blown to smithereens.

Things are worse than ever for Frankie on every level imaginable. He's biting the tail end off of a very hairy dope binge.

Although he quit the stuff ages ago... once again, he finds himself on a bit of a detour. He has taken to providing a well-known photographer with the best dope he can find. This means delving into the dangerous and unpredictable depths of East 13th Street to score dope.

Before Bulldog turned up right around the corner from Frankie's apartment, he would often score on Delancey Street. There, in an abandoned building on the corner of Delancey and Chrystie Streets, drug dealers ran a place that every junkie called The Bucket Store. The Bucket Store used an ingenious system wherein a metal painter's pail tied to a long rope was lowered from the third floor window to the sidewalk below. The customer would drop in his cash and the pail would be raised up. The dope was then lowered, with the number of bags paid for by the cash in the bucket. The next person in line would then put their money in and up the bucket would go. Frankie suspected they had the cops in their pocket, because Delancey is a main thoroughfare and the place ran trouble free for quite some time. It was open from six to nine every morning, and then they reopened at nine or ten in the evening, staying open till they ran out of dope. The Bucket Store was the most consistent operation in town.

Every junkie loves The Bucket Store! But what junkies especially love is when an unusually powerful bag of dope hits the street. Bulldog is what's really hot now. A bag like this will only be around for a short time. It's so hot that the local Bulls think so too. Bulldog was sold right around the corner from Frankie's apartment. And even though Frankie's street is only a block away and questionable at best, going around the corner to East 13th to score Bulldog is like going into a hot zone. As though the cutthroats and junkie deadbeats aren't enough to contend with, police prowl the block regularly. Frankie isn't sure why. Is someone trying to slip something by them? Refusing to pay protection maybe? Or perhaps just the opposite, and the cops are there to make sure crime levels stay low so they can continue getting payoffs from the drug dealers without bad press freaking out the Mayor, who then has to clean up the neighborhood in order to stay in office. Who knows? Either way it's a special bag. As good as street heroin gets.

The cut must be close to 50%, which, for a bag of smack sold on a NYC street in the 1980's, is phenomenal. Any more than that and junkies would be dropping like flies on a hot summer day in the kitchen of a Chinatown restaurant. Which on occasion they do. That summer, as a matter of fact almost every summer during the 1980's, a bag of dope hit the streets that would drop users left and right from overdoses. One can only wonder why a bag that strong would suddenly appear. Junkies have dozens of theories. The news would be in the papers and all over the street. For a serious junkie, it means getting your hands on as much as possible. Junkie theories are always fun to hear. Frankie is waiting in line to score on Delancey Street at six in the morning a few weeks after a really mean bag hit the streets and killed five people, one an NYU student. That dope house was promptly shut down.

"They just do it, like, you know... for advertising," suggests the transvestite addict here to score some dope.

"Advertising?" the old junkie asks.

"Yes, honey! Shit, how much of that bag did you end up buying?" They all laugh.

"I think it's the Dominicans trying to move in on the mob's action..." suggests the Daily News truck driver, also there to score. His delivery cube truck parked right there on Delancey Street with the flashers on...

"The what?" asks the transvestite.

You know, they probably ripped off a bunch of the shit and didn't know how to cut it, so it skips too many hands. And because it was stolen instead of sold the same amount of times it always gets sold, it doesn't get stepped on as much and it's just too strong for the street," the Daily News guy explains.

"It's not too strong for me, honey!" the transvestite insists. Everyone laughs.

"I don't know man, I think it's the cops trying to kill innocent junkies," says an angry new wave kid with pink hair.

"The cops?"

"Man! Why would they do that? The cops wouldn't do that, they need us on the street alive and kickin' to get, you know, raises..," says a frail older man with a Wall Street Journal under his arm.

"Well, someone is trying to kill us with that shit!" says the new wave kid.

"You're crazy!"

"Fuck you man. I know! You just don't know."

"I think we all know what's going on... I've tried to tell them... they wouldn't listen..." They all listen to the old timer. "It's the government," he says.

"What?" in unison...

Then in succession they all weigh in...

"The government?"

"What the fuck they want to kill us for?"

"You crazy!"

"You'll see... You'll see..." says the old timer, puffing on his cigarette.

All junkie theories are fascinating and are based on the same principle: Unrelenting Paranoia!

§§§§§

Frankie thinks that East 13th Street probably isn't all that much different than what a Wild West town might have been like. He has agreed to purchase five bundles of heroin for his photographer friend. Each bundle costs a hundred dollars, and as much as he likes Bernard and crazy Freddie, five hundred dollars is just too much to entrust to them. So Frankie has to traverse the dark shadows of East 13th to score the best bag in town for the photographer on his own. Squatters occupy half of the buildings on East 13th, and dealers the rest.

When he ventures into this world, everyone on the street has to check him out. Frankie learns that he has to look everyone in the eye until the tension dies... or explodes! That's what he doesn't want to happen. It becomes an art form to know just how much aggression mixed with desperation to give off with his body language and his eyes. It requires constant monitoring on Frankie's part because not enough and someone might fuck with him, too much and someone might fuck with him. It's a Stanislavski nightmare method-acting horror show. Half of the time they think Frankie is a cop.

It becomes a serious in-depth self-examination for Frankie to figure out what aspects of his personality are being accentuated by him, subconsciously to cause this association, and then change it to read 'junkie' instead of 'cop'. Frankie's not from these streets, he's from much different streets originally, and it's akin to a foreign shore for him here. No matter how much he's learned, how much he knows, how long he's been around or how quick a study he is, this isn't his backyard. And if it isn't your backyard, it isn't your backyard! Which means Frankie needs to figure himself out before anyone on the street can figure out how to treat him. For Frankie's part, he is wary of everyone.

Buying five bundles at a time for the photographer sometimes took Frankie all day and six or more trips from his apartment around the block on East 12th Street. Most junkies only score a few bags at a time. Some of them are lucky to scratch up the ten bucks just to get one bag, often resorting to violent crime to get it. To avoid costly rip-offs, the Bulldog dealers won't carry more than one or two bundles with them at a time. So, to score five bundles, Frankie has to make several trips, allowing the dealer time to re-up. And each trip around the corner is a foray into a ruthless world of desperate anarchy. Frankie decides he has to find a Bulldog dealer willing to hold five bundles and sell them to him in one fell swoop, so he doesn't have to make all those harrowing trips. After a few weeks of trying, Frankie finally convinces one of the dealers to sell him the five bundles at once. Nobody trusts anybody out here, so Frankie knows that when he does place his special order, he's going to have to wait around on the street while his order is running. Because if he's not there when the dealer returns, he'll assume Frankie flaked out on him and bring it back to Maria and the old man. Plus, the dealer would then very likely refuse to carry that much a second time. This means he has to hang around the hottest block in the East Village with five hundred dollars on him, waiting to score fifty bags of smack. Any more than that and he felt he'd have to carry a better weapon than the 8" switchblade he carries now. As it is, he's teetering on junkie paranoia. He feels like filet mignon in a pool of sharks, scoring that much dope on the street. Especially on East 13th Street. It's a trade-off. Five to ten harrowing trips into the danger zone to procure the five bundles, or one trip somewhat more intense because there's more at stake.

§§§§§

Years before meeting Baby Doll, Frankie lived on East

11th Street near Avenue B. In 1980 he was robbed at gunpoint there. His apartment was above a Latino Social Club run by a gang of lowlife criminals Frankie was constantly at odds with. One night, unbeknownst to him, three armed men hid in the dark shadows of the stairwell leading up to the next floor waiting for a chance to rip him off. He and his girlfriend had a few friends over to help with a plumbing issue the absentee landlord couldn't seem to get around to repair, and Frankie had gone out to get sandwiches and beer and for everyone. He opens the door to his apartment and enters, arms full with grocery bags. Before Frankie can put the groceries down and close the door, the thieves sneak in behind him wearing ski masks yielding 9mm's. His friends see the armed men in ski masks and crack up laughing.. "Very funny, Frankie," laughs Debbie. "Who is that, Kentor?" Terry asks. "Frankie... who is that?" asks his girlfriend giggling. His friends are under the impression that Frankie had run into some actor buddies on the street and they were pulling a prank. Frankie puts the groceries down and turns around to see what they're going on about, to find three men in ski masks pointing 9mm's at them. Frankie begins to chuckle, figuring some friends had dropped by and that they were all playing a prank on him. The three gunmen have to think Frankie and his friends are all crazy, as the people they're trying to rob at gunpoint stand around laughing at them. It isn't long before the robbers cleared up any confusion.

They made everyone get on the floor. The leader of the three thieves shoved his handgun into the back of

Frankie's head, "Where's the coca?" he asks angrily. Someone from the social club downstairs thought Frankie was dealing cocaine, because of the many visitors he had constantly dropping by. The buzzers didn't work and cellphones weren't a thing yet, so most of his friends would yell up to his window, "Hey Frankie, you home?" The lowlifes from the social club became convinced he was a drug dealer and they came to rip him off. One of the thieves held a gun on the four of them spread out on the floor, while the others ransacked the apartment. They began to break things in their frantic search, so Frankie yells at them, asking them to stop. The biggest gunman marches over and shoves his gun in Frankie's face, "I ask one more time nicely then I start to bust heads. Where is the coca?" he threatens angrily. "It's in the freezer, asshole." Frankie retorts, furious at this point. They grab the cocaine and leave.

Frankie fantasized about buying an Uzi and blowing them all away. 'Just leave me the fuck alone!' his mind raged. He did happen to have a large bag of cocaine in the freezer, it's true, but he wasn't dealing. He actually discovered it on the toilet tank in the men's room at Mary Ann's Restaurant on West 13th Street a few nights before. At the time, Mary Ann's was known as a high-end coke spot. Someone had carelessly left an ounce of high-grade cocaine on the toilet tank of the men's room. Frankie discovered it and took it home. It was the best cocaine he ever had. It was a freak coincidence and it left Frankie in the shadowy realm that exists between mad as hell and scared shitless!

Now, on East 13th Street, Frankie is counting heavily on the Big Man myth to carry him through. Freddie, the wild dope dealer, who had previously smashed up the windshield of the director's Cadillac Boise attempted to clip Boot's hubcaps for on that crazy night a year earlier, had become an ally ...when he wasn't in jail. A few bags or a few bucks whenever Frankie saw him would help keep half of the animals off his back. Frankie understood that it wasn't due to any type of loyalty or code of ethics – those days were gone with the junkies from the sixties, if they ever existed at all. No, it's simply a case of insanity by association. Everyone knows Freddie is a crazed lunatic, even by the standards of these streets. And, although it's obvious that Freddie and Frankie aren't on the same level, no one could be sure exactly what was going on. They haven't killed each other! That little bit of mystery discouraged most of the deadbeats on the street from fucking with him. Freddie dug him, for some reason unknown to Frankie. It goes back to the Big Man mythology of East 12th Street. Their street, Freddie and Frankie... East 13th Street has its own fables to deal with. It is akin to a foreign land. So Frankie relies on the legend of the Big Man fairly represented by his newly appointed ambassador, Freddie, even though he has little idea as to what it all truly alludes to.

Freddie has been a guest in Frankie's apartment on East 12th Street on several occasions. It's important to serve up a big dinner for the Ambassador at the advent of his appointment. Organize a ceremonious affair... they got high together there...

Freddie's arms would swing about uncontrollably, his eyes darting in every direction whenever he spoke. Even when he was loaded on really good smack, Freddie was up high as a kite, flyin'. Nothing would ever get him down. Really down like four or five bags of Bulldog would get you ...d.... o.... w.... n...........................

The sun is rising and Frankie has just scored some Bulldog for the photographer from around the corner. He's about to step into his apartment building on East 12th Street, when he hears Freddie's voice. Freddie always calls out with the same phrasing.

"Yo Big Man!" he yells, as he limp jumps across the street, arms waving uncontrollably.

Within speaking range, he says "... Dig... Yo Big Man! Yo, listen uh.. Hey, how ya doin? Alright?" Frankie nods his head.

"Yeah... Hey, you know Morris?"

Frankie gives him a quizzical look...

"Morris? You know... the big dude down by Avenue C?" Freddie insists.

"You mean the guy with the anaconda near 11th Street?" Frankie asks.

"Ana-who!?! No man, look, the fat dude with the big hat? You know, the other guy," he says his eyes darting around, bouncing off the doorway a few times.

"Okay, yeah, I know who you mean. The big guy near 6th Street, on the corner with the dog, right?" asks Frankie, fairly sure he's got the right guy.

"Dog!?! What fuckin' dog? Aint no dog... Yo, for a dude with schoolin' and shit, you know, you can be one stupid muthafucka, Big Man! I'm sorry to tell you... But MAN!!! Look... ...the guy with the big hat. The John Wayne number and the... the... the.... whatsamacallit?"

"Oh yeah... that dude," Frankie says, in sudden realization.

"Yeah!" he says, out of breath from the huge effort. "Damn... I knew you knew, Big Man. Check it out... He's got the good bag, man. You don't got to go to those Bulldog muthafuckas!"

"What's wrong with Bulldog? I love Bulldog, Freddie, it's a good bag, man... right around the corner..."

"Fuck them!" Freddie demands.

"You have some kind of problem with them?" Frankie asks, interested...

"Yeah... Shit, Big Man... Look, try one of the bags, man... from this dude... you won't be sorry, man..."

"I really like the Dog, man, but here, buzz me." He hands Freddie a twenty and looks at his face a moment. One eye is oozing something and is a bit swollen and there are scars on his face Frankie never noticed before. It was one of those moments when you look at someone you think you know and realize they could be someone else. Frankie enters his apartment trying to shake off the feeling.

He sits at his desk and lays the five bundles on the table. He looks at them for a moment, relieved. He sits down and begins to unravel every bag he bought for the photographer. Fifty bags, one at a time. He thought back to the time he would get twelve in a bundle, the two as a bonus when you bought a whole bundle. Not anymore. Frankie thought, 'Gee, maybe Freddie's right. I'll have to ask him if the dude with the John Wayne hat does the bonus bags.' But that would be the last time Frankie saw Freddie. And as much as it appears Freddie has disappeared for good this time, Frankie holds on to his birth certificate and some court papers Freddie had given him for safekeeping. I suppose you could say they were pals.

Frankie empties a little less than half the contents of each bag onto his desk into a huge pile of dope. This is his cut, sort of a shipper's tax. Carrying charges, Sydney Greenstreet called it in Casablanca... Frankie knows that it is a practice as old as trade itself ...a bit off the top for the men crossing the desert or the ocean sea. He carefully removes the tape from the little blue wax bag, pours a little less than half of the dope out then folds the bag the exact same way and tapes it back together. It's tedious work, but naturally he gets off first, so it's not that bad. Bulldog is high quality street heroin, so he doesn't feel so bad clipping half for himself. In fact, he feels it is his responsibility to make sure that the amateurs who will eventually use this stuff don't get too strong a hit and overdose. Besides, Bulldog is very difficult to obtain. You have to show tracks and know someone they trusted to even get near the Bulldog dealers. But even before that, you have to meet the stringers who would check out your needle tracks and listen to the story of who you know and how you know them, before the old man or Maria would even consider selling to you. They, of course would then have to see your tracks, listen to the story of who you know, and how you know them, first hand. The special person, usually a lowlife scumbag, is someone in jail or dead now anyway, but that's the way it is.

Frankie is high as a kite back in the safety of his apartment, busily procuring his carrying charges, when the phone rings. He listens through the answering machine. It's the photographer trying to find out why it's taking so long to get his dope. 'Fuck him!' Frankie decides... 'I'm the one dodging the cops, cutthroats and hustler pieces of shit all over the damn place... let him fucking wait.'

"Hello?" Frankie says, picking up the receiver.

The machine squeals and whistles...

"Hold on," Frankie says.

"Yeah?"

"What the fuck is going on?" screams the photographer.

"Hey, how're ya doing?" Frankie answers, not investing in an argument.

"Did you score?" he asks anxiously.

"Yeah, I fucking scored... It took all morning 'cause Maria was more paranoid than usual, the cops were stopping anybody who walked down the sidewalk, and every junkie in New York City got up with the fishermen to score today, hours ahead of me, so Bulldog had to re-up and the whole street was waiting around. It was a fucking dope fiend convention, with every junkie hooker in Manhattan offering to suck you off behind a garbage can or a doorway for ten bucks. It was nuts, man, I'm telling you. You don't know what's going on out there." Frankie explains, just so the photographer doesn't take it all for granted, which he will anyway. Now Frankie is into another set of tactics to deal with this guy. A completely different style with its own brand of particulars, yet basically the same deal.

"I'm in my car now. I'll swing over!" the pushy photographer says.

"Who are you with?" Frankie inquires.

"Boise..." he answers knowingly.

"Yeah? Ask him if he needs any hubcaps?" Frankie smiles.

Through the phone Frankie can hear, "Hey, Reno wants to know if you need any hubcaps?"

Frankie laughs. "Where are you?" he asks.

"I'm on Fifth Avenue and ...Boise, what street are we on ...49th? 49th Street!"

"Great. Come on by," Frankie says.

He knows he has plenty of time to finish clipping all the bags before the photographer could get to his apartment from 49th Street. This routine went on for months. Sometimes the photographer had to send his photo assistants to a fleabag hotel to meet Frankie's connections to score. Something Frankie would arrange when he was out of town. Often it was Herman, the one-eyed junkie from Spanish Harlem who was Frankie's one-time neighbor at The Carlton Arms hotel. The photo assistants would flip a wig when they saw these places ...dingy, smelly, sad hotels full of thieves, hookers and forgotten people trying their best to forget. Frankie would receive word from the photographer that his assistants would return from these excursions into Frankie's drug netherworld still shaking in their boots ...how could he do that to an innocent kid from the Midwest. Next time he sees them Frankie berates the assistants for their girlish behavior... they need to man up and stop making such a big deal out of nothing... In truth, however, sending those young decent inexperienced assistants into Frankie's world served as a fair measure to exactly what this world he has come to make his own actually was. Something he wasn't readily disposed to acknowledge.

§§§§§

Frankie knows he's sinking. He's been sinking for some time, yet it hits him suddenly like a ton of bricks. He's got another bad habit. 'I have to clean out! I have to do it this time! I've got to at least try!' he tells himself.

He's in a bar on Avenue A around the corner from his house. It's his birthday and two of his old pals are buying him drinks. Neither of them has a clue about Frankie's fondness for heroin.

"I've blown it!" Frankie mutters, close to tears.

His friends are truly worried about him.

He sucks back the rest of a double Bushmills. He looks over at his two buddies.

"Frankie man, ya gotta chill out," says Bart.

"I can't," he mutters, as tears stream down his face.

Tim buys another round. Frankie lifts it from the bar slowly and notices that his hand is shaking. He started drinking when he awoke that morning, yet he can't lose the shakes. He's avoiding getting high on heroin because he can't do it any longer... he just can't! He doesn't want to drink anymore either, but he has to.

"Reno man, you're not that bad off, you've..."

"What are you talking about?" Frankie yelps, interrupting. "My whole life is over! I blew it! I have nothing to show for thirty-three years on this planet!" He downs another double.

Frankie looks around the bar. The place is filled with happy people, hanging out, drinking and having a few laughs. He's in the same room as them, leaning against the same bar, being served by the very same bartender, but he's a million miles away and there isn't a thing he can do about it. He can't turn it off ...Frankie's too far gone... the dread... the remorse... the panic... the mortal terror, desperation and fear slam his heart like the relentless surf of a wild ocean... His mind is frazzled. The booze isn't working anymore. He's been drinking all day, but his mind continues to churn, filled with worry and regret. There is no escaping his predicament. He's as lost as he can ever be, and he knows it.

He also knows of a way out.

But he doesn't allow himself to think it.

"Here, have another drink," Tim says, pushing a double in front of him.

"Thanks, Tim," he says and drinks it down.

"Here," Tim says, "take this." He hands Frankie a couple of twenties.

"I've got to split," he says. "Ease up man, take it slow." He pats Frankie on the back and leaves.

Frankie turns to Bart. "I've got to go, too," he says. "Sorry I'm such a mess."

"Frank, you're having some dark days. We all get 'em, Try to relax. Maybe you should ease up on the drinking," he advises.

The comment strikes Frankie as very comical but he doesn't have the wherewithal to laugh. He has attempted for weeks to control the intake of alcohol to no avail. Three weeks ago, his last fix, he promised himself he wouldn't have a drink before sunset! But he couldn't do it. The next day he promised himself he wouldn't drink before five. No dice. By the third day he was promising himself he wouldn't drink before noon. Noon! A virtual impossibility... he would wake up and grab a bottle.

His head aches. His mind is heavy and fuzzy. He can't think straight. In fact he can barely speak. He feels an intense need to move. To get outta there... His mind reels. 'Go! Walk! Anywhere... nowhere... this way, no that way! Where am I? Oh... Bart's here! Shit! What do I say? Ummm... Should I score some dope? No!!! I've got to go home... I've got to go home... I've got to go home...'

"Hey Frank!" The sound echoes in his head. "Frankie!"

Hunh!?! What is that sound? Jesus, help me!

"Frankie, man! Hey!" shouts Bart, shaking him by the shoulders. Frankie's drink has spilled and his head and arm are soaking in it. He lifts his head and begins to focus.

"Yeah? Hmf... Oh Bart... Shit..." Frankie wipes his face with a few bar napkins and says, "Let's get out of here."

They walk outside. Frankie's bouncing off the walls.

"I'll see ya, pal. I gotta go," Frankie says. Then he just walks off. Bart watches him walk away. He shakes his head in sorrow, turns and walks down the street alone. Frankie has nowhere to go, but he just can't be near anyone. He walks in the direction of his apartment a total wreck. Home is the most depressing place on the planet for him right now, yet that's where he is walking ...mindlessly. Halfway down the block, a slick looking dope dealer he's seen around pitches him.

"Yo, Blue Steel," he says slyly under his breath, looking up at Frankie.

Frankie stops walking abruptly, grabs him by the front of his jacket, lifts him off the ground, and throws him against the roll-down steel gate of the Ecuadorian restaurant up the block from his apartment. Frankie sneers at the dope dealer, his face inches away. Holding him off the ground, he shoves him with great force up against the gate, in thrusts that mirror what he's saying.

"Don't you ever fucking pitch me again, you muthafucker! I don't get high anymore, all right? You little fuck, I'll kill you! I'll fucking kill you," Frankie menaces.

"Yo... Big Man! I'm sorry man! Yo! Alright!" squeals the dope dealer suspended in mid air.

Frankie can feel him squirming in his grasp. Only it's as though it's happening to two other people.

"Agh shit!" Frankie says in dismay. He drops him to the ground and stumbles up the block towards his home. The dealer watches him walk away, shaking his head as he tucks his shirt back in and fixes his hair.

In the simplest of terms, I suppose you could say Frankie is having a nervous breakdown. A more generically obscure medical or psychological classification has yet to be created. 'We don't really know exactly what's the matter with you, but it's not good'. What is happening to Frankie is more than just a nervous breakdown, for the simple reason that it involves more than just his nerves. He is frazzled to the core. A complete mental, emotional, physical and spiritual meltdown more accurately describes his condition at this moment.

He goes home, finishes whatever booze he has in the house, and passes out without a fix. The next day he wakes up to the loneliest world he has ever known. Terror fills him. His apartment is cold. The walls are gray. Everything is wrong. There's no booze in the house. He's shaking, and very afraid. He reaches for the phone. His mind reels... 'Who can I possibly call? There's no one. There's no one to call. Who would understand?' He can't think of anyone he can call with the news that, that... that what? What is happening? He knows, yet he doesn't know. There's no clear definition for him. No absolution. He can't stop shaking. Tears begin to stream down his face. Frankie feels as though his life has just ended. That his three minutes are up... He's run out of quarters at the phone booth of life and his call is about to be interrupted. Now there's nothing left to do but hang up. It's either that, or venture even deeper into the abyss. His life is too dark now however, any farther down and... he'd rather be dead!

He leaves his apartment building and walks the streets aimlessly. He walks and he walks...

Due to some lost and confused synapse of the brain his conscious mind cannot fathom, he enters a street then just as quickly turns and goes the other way. He walks by a liquor store and, in a bizarre hallucination that could just as easily be from a Disney cartoon, the entire liquor store leaps out at him in the form of a hundred brass horns. The volume is astounding. It knocks him clear into the middle of the street, where a city bus is barreling in his direction. The driver blows the horn and slams on his brakes. It's too close! There's no way it can slow down fast enough. Frankie looks up, sees the bus coming straight at him, then leaps out of the way just in time. A young woman sees it and screams, causing everyone on the sidewalk to stop and stare at him as he stumbles about. Wow, he thinks. He waves them off and begins to walk again. He looks back over his shoulder and a little wheeze of a horn from the liquor store blows a friendly note at him. He shakes his head in disbelief and continues to walk away. He ends up at Father Demo Park on Carmine and Bleecker Streets near Sixth Avenue.

Frankie has seen them all morning. Sitting in doorways. Crouched over park benches. Crashed out on subway steps ...everywhere. And now here he was, the one who is going to touch him. He looks as though he could be a hundred years old, but he's probably only fifty. His clothes are tattered. His hair unkempt and his pale blue eyes are glassy. He reaches out his dry, soiled hand in a call for loose change. Frankie looks into the man's eyes. The last tear made its exit a long time ago. They stand there a moment just staring into each other's eyes. The rest of the world becomes a barrage of fleeting images, zipping by him and this stranger at increasing velocity. Frankie can sense other people walking by and cars driving up Sixth Avenue, but they are more like wisps of shadow that sound like buzzing bees. The man is the only thing in focus. It feels as though they are stuck in a netherworld, a time-lapse or a parallel dimension of some sort. Frankie gazes into the man's face and sees the future. His future. The man is Frankie, in twenty years. He is the Grim Reaper! Frankie has met the Grim Reaper and he wants to leave. However, he is frozen in place and can't move a muscle. He struggles, with great difficulty. Heaving and grunting, he tries desperately to release himself from this mysterious supernatural grip. Then, with more effort and courage than it took to make his very first step in this world, Frankie lifts his leg and moves. It may have only been an inch. It might have only been half an inch. But it was enough. Suddenly, he's back in real time. He has returned to the world of living, breathing mortals. It was a painful transition, but the pain decreases a little bit with each step that he takes, and he's glad to be back. People take on full form again and reflect sunlight in color. Frankie walks up Sixth Avenue.

He's still a bit numb, and so he's unclear as to what exactly just happened, but something has changed. Something's different. He may not know it yet, but something very crucial has been altered. A cosmic shift has occurred deep in his psyche. He has found a glimmer of hope. He doesn't dare look back either. He knows in every absolute sense that, if he did, he would turn into a pillar of salt.

XIV

Warnings

When the sun sets, who doth not look for night?
Shakespeare, Richard III

When Frankie was a boy, his father owned a construction company, and when he reached the age of nine or ten, his dad would take him along on weekend tours of his job sites to show him the ropes.

At some point every Saturday they would end up at a large industrial yard. Most were situated on eerily lifeless dead-end side streets in half-forgotten industrial sections along the outer boroughs of New York City. Often alongside an odiferous body of sulfured water, usually a canal, an inlet or bay... like Jamaica Bay, the odors of which, in some areas at low tide, could make even a seasoned adventurer gag. As they drove along, Frankie would watch the sunlight shimmer off of the oil-slicked water in hypnotic dances of light. He would stare at these reflections, losing himself in them. He wondered how something that smelled so awful could be so beautiful. As if this beauty were an act of defiance on the part of the water, which struggled to be magnificent and vibrant despite the sulfur, oils, and garbage that had been forced upon it. Frankie felt akin to this water in ways that cannot be described. During those boyhood years he felt as though it were trying to speak to him.

His father would pull the car right up the middle of one of these industrial yards, past the barbed wire topped gates of the standard dilapidated Cyclone fence, and turn off the engine. Trucks and all manner of equipment would be stacked in bits and pieces everywhere he looked. Some of it piled as high as three story buildings. Dense dusted grease covered everything. The ground was an earthen sponge of it. Weeds and trees struggled against it wherever they could.

They would usually need to speak with one of the men who either ran the place or just sort of hung around looking for work. Invariably, as they entered these yards, a lone wolf of a dog would raise its head lazily as though to do so caused it pain. It seemed to Frankie, at the time, that they were simply too covered with dusty grease to make it over to howl at them. He left them alone, those mangy yard dogs, as much because of the pity and sadness he felt up close in their presence, as due to fear of the ferocious dog that, he knew from direct experience, still lurked beneath the hindering layers of grease, sawdust and metal filings which had now become a permanent part of its coat.

"C'mon-a-son, wake up!" his father would rant.

His father was well aware that he wasn't asleep, but Frankie had a tendency to daydream, and his father knew that a loud sharp voice was required to draw him back into the same world he was in. Frankie preferred self-propelled illusions to the ache-filled and limiting world occupied by most adults ...performing circus clowns and his Uncle Cosmos excluded.

His alluring fantasies of being all-powerful and unafraid drove a compelling resolve that told him his needs surpassed all other events worldwide, and were challenged constantly by every authority figure he encountered, to no avail. He could never be convinced that what was referred to as growing up had any real advantages. Frankie would spend uncountable periods of time in one of his invented worlds, inspired by the many tales he had read, seen or heard about in stories like 'The Adventures of Huck Finn', 'Lost Horizon' or 'West Side Story' and 'The Lives of A Bengal Lancer' (how he loved that book), or 'Gunga Din', 'Peter Pan'... yes! That was big. Peter Pan! He took a lot of heat for that one...

How often his dad would point to some piece of equipment lying on the ground nearby, Frankie cannot recount.

"Ya see a dat ting ova dere... put dat in de car," he'd say nonchalantly.

"Thing, dad. Thing, not ting," Frankie would say.

"Thinga," his father manages with difficulty.

Frankie's father was an Italian immigrant and English was his second language. It was Frankie's job, along with his brother and sisters, to help his father learn proper pronunciation of English words.

When he was in the first grade, his mother had insisted that Frankie let his father help him with his homework. His father attempted to aid Frankie with a pronunciation and slowly convinced him to pronounce 'red' with a roaring Euro-trash roll of the tongue. Rrrrred! Allowing the tongue to sputter, making a sort of engine noise preceding the actual 'red' part of the word. "Rrrrrred! ...Rrrrrred!" His father insisted. "Try it, I betta you teach, she knows! Hunh?!..."

The next day in class, Frankie gave it a loving attempt.

"What," the teacher asked, "are you doing?"

"Rrrrred," he repeated proudly, "Rrrrred!"

"Frankie, what's wrong? Are you feeling alright?" the teacher inquired. His classmates were mystified. Some even laughed! Enough of that, he thought. So everyone in the family decided to help his father learn English pronunciations to English words, instead.

"Ova dere," his father says impatiently. "That ting... thinga, ova dere...see?" Frankie walks over to the large godforsaken greasy metal object his father is referring to.

"What, this?" he asks.

"Yeah... yeah, it's a mine. I left him here lasta week..." Looking about he adds, "dona leta nobody see, hunh?"

"This thing is yours?" young Frankie asks.

"Uddy up! Uddy up!" his father screams, looking around to see who might be watching.

Frankie lifts the heavy greasy object and carries it to the car. "Hurry," he mutters, "Hurry, not uddy..."

"Justa put 'im in the trunk! Huddy up, dammit!" His father yells, losing patience, still looking around furtively and handing Frankie the car keys. "Dad, if this is yours, why are we rushing around like this?" he asks innocently, dragging the heavy object into the trunk.

"Why! Why! You always aska why! Just do it... Maronne! What's amatta wid you? Kids today... you tell 'em to do asometin' and dey don do it..." I don know..."

 So, Frankie would take the greasy, essential piece of equipment for some such thing-a-ma-jig and wrestle it into the trunk of the car.

He had little idea exactly what these heavy oily things did. All he knew is that they needed them and that either someone wasn't returning them after having borrowed them, or his father had left them somewhere and they would, by good fortune, turn up in one of these yards. After a while, of course, he figured it out. His father would explain that so much stuff was stolen from his job sites, stealing stuff back everywhere they went was the only way he could stay in business. It was just the way the world was. It was completely justifiable.

" ...Everybody shes'a steala from me! Dona kidda youself. You canna trust ano-abody in dis a-world," he insisted. "Rememba! Believe nothing of whata you hear and half a whata you see and den... maybe!!! ....You mighta get a glimpse of a da troot!"

"Truth!" Frankie says. "Trut-th. Troot... no... Trutha..." his father tries. This approach to life became second nature to Frankie. After a while he began to feel that no one gave a damn, and the world was going to shit. That this is the way everyone did things. It was his introduction to politics. He hated his father for making him drag stuff into the trunk of the car or out of a store, for their foraging wasn't simply limited to construction yards. But admired him too, as someone able to make such a self-possessed decision about his place in a world Frankie was only beginning to misunderstand. Yet, how is he supposed to deal with this on a personal level? By the time he reached the age of thirteen, he was convinced that life only made sense in his imagination, and that is where he intended to live.

XV

Spilt Milk

"...and damn'd be him that first cries, "Hold, enough!"
Shakespeare: Macbeth

Often, while growing up, Frankie was admonished for spilling milk, something it would appear he did often. Some things never change. Some things aren't meant to. They are the things we must accept about ourselves, and the world at large, in order to move forward. There are moments in Frankie's life when he is faced with the choice of banging his head against a brick wall or moving forward by searching the wall and finding the gate ...or any reasonable point of least resistance in order to get to the other side. I suppose it's fair to say, paraphrasing words of considerable wisdom picked up somewhere, that rational men change with their environments in an attempt to adapt and co-exist with that environment, whereas irrational men try to change their surroundings to suit their wants. It would seem that very little progress would have occurred throughout history, had there not been a wealth of irrational men scurrying about banging their heads against the wall. For better or worse is the question.

Some things never change. Then again, some things aren't meant to change. They are there waiting for us, like a bus. Suddenly there it is. You step on, pay your fare and it takes you where you're supposed to go. And

when you get there, you know that's where you're
supposed to be.

XVI

Just What He'd Always Wanted

"So long? Nay, then, let the devil wear black, for I'll have a suit of sables."
Shakespeare: Hamlet

Frankie lived and worked at the Carolton Arms Hotel the first time he did heroin. The Carolton Arms is an elegant name for a hellhole no self-respecting individual would end up in. But that is where he ended up, all right. 'Does it beseem thee to weave cloth of Devil's dust instead of true wool?' It did for Frankie. In fact, it was better than the real thing ...for a while. It was just what he'd always wanted.

A rocker chick bartender who worked in downtown strip joints and after-hours clubs lived there at the time. Her boyfriend was a drug dealer ...a middle-aged Puerto Rican gentlemen from the Lower East Side who everyone called Rico. He introduced Frankie to heroin. Rico would visit the rocker chick at the hotel almost daily. One day he asked Frankie if he got high. Frankie said yeah. Rico motioned for Frankie to follow him, which he did. They walked up the lobby stairway half a flight and Rico pulled out a folded up piece of paper about the size of a chewing gum wrapper. He took out some white powder and let Frankie sniff it. Nothing was the same after that. Frankie found the escape he'd been looking for since he was tossed off of that merry-go-round when he was eight years old. There is an irony in the fact that Frankie's first heroin was had on a stairway...

§§§§§

How quickly the days passed on heroin. Only, Frankie got hooked. It took a long time to get over his first heroin addiction ...those days didn't pass nearly as quickly. He entered a methadone detoxification program in Spanish Harlem. They started him at forty milligrams. After a few months he whittled down to five. A few weeks of that and he was ready to go to ground zero. He didn't sleep for months after he left that place.

Frankie may be a junkie, but he's also a Renaissance man armed with a plethora of talent and daring in every artistic discipline he puts his hands to. He scores an amazing commission as a sculptor carving a dozen life-sized relief sculptures of classic automobiles out of polystyrene. They are to become a part of the façade of an Art Deco style hotel in Miami, Florida. Once completed and installed, it will appear that they were carved right from the walls of the building. He is given a large empty space to use as his art studio in the huge six-story elevator car garage on the west side of Manhattan that houses the over fifty classic cars. He imagines he'll be there around six months carving them. Frankie's still shaking like a leaf half of the time and has to drink a lot of gin to lose the shakes so he can work. But the sculptures are turning out fantastic and he's pretty happy about it. Of course, switching from dope to methadone then to booze is like playing musical chairs on the Hindenburg, but at the time it seemed to the only solution.

A week or two into the commission he discovers Alcoholics Anonymous. With the help of AA he finally gets sober and is able to stay that way for a while. After a full day of carving a 55 Chevy, Frankie strolls down 10th Avenue on his way home to his apartment in Chelsea. Enjoying the orange glow of a sunset-filled sky, an unexpected sensation of warmth engulfs him. Soon his entire body is humming in near ecstasy. It's an astonishingly delightful sensation for Frankie ...without a fix or a drink! The profound nature of the feeling he's experiencing is nothing less than overwhelming. He stops and finds a nearby telephone pole to brace himself against, absolutely bewildered by the sheer intensity of it. The dazzling sensation leaves him all but incapacitated as it triggers a deep-rooted physiological memory in his body he thought lost forever. Motionless and all alone, he weeps from the emotional ferocity of the experience. The natural function of his endorphin glands kicked in. Common terminology would call it a jogger's high or after-glow. For years, Frankie's sidestepping every feeling he could, through artificial means, prevented this from ever occurring. But here it is, and it makes him weep like a child.

§§§§§

With most of the insane behavior behind him, Frankie begins to breathe easy again. He secures an amazing position as a director-cameraman for a Portuguese documentary aboard a Portuguese Tall Ship. The 100-meter sailing vessel is a three-mast barque named Sagres, and is beyond wonderful! For Frankie it brings to mind the Old Spice ship on the bottles he had received every year for Christmas from his grandmother ever since he started to shave at the tender age of thirteen.

He is to sail with the Portuguese Navy for an event Opsail put together called 'The Columbus Race'... a race designed to emulate Columbus' journey to the new world. They will set sail in Genoa, Italy stopping in Old San Juan, Puerto Rico, New York, Newport and Boston. Nearly every country in the world with a navy operates one of these magnificent schooners, and the ship that reaches Boston first wins the race. It is a celebration of Columbus' claim of the Americas 500 years earlier. A celebration mainly for white people, Frankie imagined... who else would celebrate something like that? Certainly not the Taino Indians of the Caribbean. That aside, Frankie is exhilarated for the opportunity to venture out to the open sea. The great Ocean Sea, Columbus called it.

Whatever else one might say about Columbus, he had a wonderful adventurous streak in him. Frankie has admired all the great adventurers ever since he was a child, and can hardly believe his good fortune.

Being hundreds of miles out to sea is a revelation for Frankie. One late afternoon he finds himself alone on the aft deck gazing out onto the vast ocean, awestruck by the sheer majesty of it. For the first time in many years his mind isn't racing. He experiences a peace he had previously known only after a good fix of dope. The ship rides a healthy breeze in the tropics, headed north for New York City having left Puerto Rico less than a week before. Standing there, Frankie becomes somewhat hypnotized by the water and a sudden urge grabs hold of him. Without warning, he is overwhelmed by a nearly uncontrollable desire to leap into the ocean. The ship has a good clip going too... about eighteen knots, and he would surely have been lost forever. It's very strange, because the impulse to leap is not the result of a thought process, but rather a fiercely powerful physical urge.

Frankie had heard of this phenomenon. People out to sea for extended periods of time become deeply affected by the hypnotic quality of the water, and finally leap in, as though bestowing on her the ultimate offering, their lives. But it is more than the mere hypnotic quality, because there is no mental decision involved whatsoever, as there would be for someone deciding to commit suicide. The impulse to leap into the ocean seems more the result of a deep-seated subconscious physiological memory of the water in one's body, 60% of which is water. Including intracellular fluids, this means our body is actually close to 98% water-based liquid. Liquid that is compelled to rejoin the massive body of water of the ocean, like a magnet or a biological intelligence of some kind. It's why there are telephones along the entire walkway overlooking Niagara Falls. People freeze up or unexpectedly express a desire to leap in, and someone must invariably call for help. Frankie is holding on to the railing with all his might, astonished at the extreme physical urge to leap into the ocean that he's experiencing. Frankie is quite suddenly and unexpectedly engaged in a battle of wits between his body and his mind The subconscious mind, but a battle nonetheless. His body is nearly trembling when a voice breaks the spell. It's Duarte.

One of the six journalists aboard, Duarte was a focador in Portugal for years until the age of twenty-two. Focadors are the men in Portuguese bullfights that jump onto the bull, holding on to his horns, risking life and limb in an attempt to confuse and tire him out. What a job! Frankie asks if he'd met many women because of it. Duarte admitted that, yes, there are many women who find it alluring, but insisted that the women were merely a fringe benefit. That it was truly the thoughtless thrill of it that attracted him. A man thing, Frankie imagined.

Frankie and the other journalists, like the naval officers and cadets aboard, have access to the aft deck and will often enjoy this hour in the afternoon there. Frankie is sleeping less and less at sea. It seems five hours is plenty. And, as there are huge blocks of time with not much to do, he would fraternize before dinner, exchanging stories with some of the officers and journalists. One of the journalists is Salvatore. Old Salvatore is leery of everyone, and not very engaging. He has little respect for where they are, it seems, and remains as inconspicuous as possible. He'd written about everything on the planet and is world-weary. He is bored. Frankie has nothing in common with him. Salvatore is on his last story and so old he would often fall asleep right at the dinner table. Dinner table!?! Unlike the enlisted sailors who dine cafeteria-style in the bow, Frankie, Joao, the producer who had hired him, and the other journalists dined with the officers in a dining room designed for ten people and lined in teak. Which, with its round portholes positioned just above sea level, is truly magnificent. The Sagres employs very clever 2" high place setting borders that protect each officer's dinner plates from sliding away. Used only when needed in especially rough seas, the contraption folds into a compact hinged storable unit when not in use. Like all things on an A-Class naval sailing vessel, there is a place for everything and everything in its place. These devices keep everyone's dinner plates where they belong, without having to hold onto them when the ship heaves to and fro. Frankie loves the fact that he doesn't have to tip his soup bowl to get to all of the delicious Portuguese codfish stew often served on board. The swells do that for him. He simply places his spoon in the bowl and the ocean does the rest, as it rocks the ship back and forth filling his spoon every time. For the duration of the journey, Frankie has the privilege of dining with the Captain once a week in his private round-table dining room. The captain is wise, graceful and elegant, with the appearance of a storybook sea captain. Graying beard and everything.

Then there is Joseph, the reason for Duarte's excursion to the aft deck to have a word with Frankie that afternoon.

"That leetle faggot," Duarte says in a loud whisper.

Frankie has been on board long enough to know exactly whom Duarte is talking about. Joseph is the Portuguese radio correspondent. An obnoxious little creep who, every night, would enter the radio room on board and transmit three minutes to the mainland about what happened that day. Little patriotic encapsulations for the folks back home in Lisbon. He's not only the most boring fellow Frankie has ever met, but he's also a pest about it.

"If he says one more word to me I will keel heem," Duarte rages under his breath, his face so close Frankie could taste the cordial he just drank. Duarte looks about as he's speaking to make sure no one can overhear what he's saying. Frankie felt he truly might. That one day Joseph would just disappear. Duarte had that kind of serious edge to him. Frankie is glad he and Duarte have become friends. In fact, Frankie feels Duarte is one of the warmest human beings he has ever met. A very large part of Frankie loves Duarte. It is the kind of closeness you had as a child toward your closest pal.

One of the officers, Phillipé, is the Head Navigator, as well as the Public Relations Officer on board. Frankie is welcome to visit with Phillipé on the bridge to learn about astral navigation and the like, which he does often. Although the ship is equipped with GPS and radar, the rules of the race allow only the use of navigational technology that was available circa 1492. All the ships in the race are limited to the tools Columbus had at his disposal in order to navigate their way from Genoa, Italy, to Puerto Rico, New York, Newport and Boston, the final destination. This means using a sextant, astrolabe and a fascinating spherical star-mapped device about the size of a soft ball encased in a small wooden box called a celestial armillary globe. Being such a significant contribution to Portuguese discoveries during the Age of Exploration. the flag of Portugal features a pronounced armillary sphere. Among other things, this brilliant contraption, dating back to the Ancient Greeks, allows the navigator to determine the declination of the sun. As all sailors know, the sun sets in a different spot on the horizon each day. If you follow the sun west during the winter, it will take you to a different place than it would were you to follow it in the summer. Because of this, sailors can only find true east, west north or south by determining the declination of the sun.

Visiting with Phillipé on the bridge, Frankie peers into the radar screen and notices a large fuzzy white patch in the direction in which they are heading. He asks Phillipé about it. "Ah, Frankie, zis is very bad weather. A very large system it looks like, too."

Frankie looks at the screen. "Oh yeah? We're heading straight for it," says Frankie. He looks at Phillipé and asks, "Shouldn't we go east or west to avoid it?"

Phillipé chuckles at his remark then says, "Frankie, we

are here ...see?" Phillipé points to their location, "...and New York is here..." He points to New York on the radar screen, "We must go though zis weather to reach New York."

'These guys are crazy!' Frankie says to himself, looking at the screen.

About a week later they enter the Bermuda Triangle. For Frankie, being in the Bermuda Triangle is beyond fascinating. He keeps an eye out for Amelia Earhart and the many lost ships and airplanes that have disappeared here over the years.

A few days into the Triangle, at two in the morning, a loud violent boom throws Frankie out of his bunk. He wakes up on the floor with the alarms ringing and the ship keeling and bobbing violently. Bouncing on the ocean like a cork in a washing machine.

They've hit severe squalls. The storm quickly evolves into a full-blown hurricane. Something Frankie could never have prepared himself for. That little fuzzy white patch he saw on the radar screen a week earlier is tame compared to the reality of it now! The ship gets knocked around violently. He gets dressed as quickly as he can, while being tossed around like a ragdoll. He needs to capture this!

He begins to make his way up to the sergeant's quarters just off the bridge, where he keeps his camera gear. On the gangway, halfway up, amidst the chaos of sailors dashing about madly in emergency mode, wind and rain howling, lightning and thunder crashing, stands a smallish sailor resembling Peter Lorre. He leans against the gangway wall, a cigarette dangling from his mouth, calm as a cucumber. It stops Frankie dead in his tracks. He's astonished not only at how calm this one sailor is compared to everyone else on board, but that the cigarette dangling from his mouth has a nearly inch long ash on it. The ship is bobbing and heaving violently. Everyone on board is in overdrive dealing with the storm, yet here is this lone sailor resembling Peter Lorre, mysteriously calm. They stand there for a moment staring at one another. Finally the sailor takes the cigarette between his index and middle finger, flicks the extraordinarily long ash, looks Frankie in the eyes and cryptically, in what can only be described as a Bavarian accent, says, "It is very dangerous." Frankie has no idea who he is. He doesn't remember having seen him before ...but then there are more than two hundred men aboard. He grabs ahold of his senses and rushes up the gangway to mid-ship, shaking his head. 'Who was that guy?' he says to himself. The scene on deck is utter mayhem as the wind howls ferociously in what are now forty-foot seas. The angry rain whips at his face, while magnificent lightning flashes light up the scene.

Being thrown about savagely, Frankie makes it to the sergeant's quarters without busting his head open, mounts his camera in the waterproof housing he'd brought along, and begins shooting whatever he can. Sailors brave the storm, climbing the masts in order to reef in the monster-sized square-rigged sails. The largest of the 24 sails are over 40' wide. The ship was at full sail with rudder out on a reach, clipping along at twenty knots, and when the big winds came, there was nowhere left to go. Frankie shoots video the entire time, even though it is the dead of night, and storming ferociously with severe seas, fierce winds and heavy rain. The sound is amazing. And the fact that the only visuals that come through from that footage occur when lightning flashes light up the scene to capture sailors rushing by or hauling sheets in flashes of action make it very exciting footage!

At dawn, five hours later, there is a slight lull in the storm. The sailors have gotten the ship under as near control as is possible in these extreme conditions, so Frankie collects himself for a moment, hanging on tightly as the ship continues to heave in the wild raging of the sea below. 'These are truly courageous men,' he thinks to himself. 'Talk about a man thing!' He wonders what Willie the biker back on Avenue A would have to say about these amazing sailors. Or Chicky Zilner! He stands there for a moment, awestruck being two hundred miles out to sea in a hurricane and thinks, 'Who's better than me?' He smiles as a memory flashes through his mind when he would ride his bicycle from his apartment in the East Village to Tribeca, where he sometimes works in a commercial production house producing television commercials. Some mornings he would spot two old winos seated together on a park bench at Allen Street Park. One of the winos would guzzle some cheap wine then pass the bottle to his pal and say, "Who's better than us?" The other wino takes the bottle, guzzles the rest of it, looks over at the first wino and answers, "Nobody." Frankie would stop and pretend to adjust his bicycle seat or tie his shoes when he spotted them, just to watch this display of what he likes to call wino brotherly love. Frankie still has one foot in each world it seems, because of all the thoughts that might have popped into his head at that moment, 200 miles out to sea during a hurricane in the Bermuda Triangle, it is those two winos on that decrepit old bench in Allen Street Park that come to mind.

The sea continues to rage as the crew grabs a short respite, having frantically worked to secure all the sails. Frankie stands there for a moment, bedazzled by this once in a lifetime experience and says, "Who's better than me?" He chuckles and a big smile comes to his face. Then he adds, "Nobody." Frankie stands there alone holding on tightly, laughing aloud at the irony of it, when the great Captain approaches. He looks at Frankie with what can only be called a sweet affection. The other journalists are cowering in their bunks, but here is Frankie on deck, capturing the heroic efforts of the captain's crew on camera, laughing out loud to himself. One can only imagine what the captain must be thinking. Whatever it is, it's brought a smile to his face, even though the ship continues to get knocked around savagely by the storm. Working to keep his balance, the Captain pulls something wrapped in wax paper out of his pocket and hands it to Frankie, who is still giddy from the 'Nobody' line.

"Here," the Captain says, holding the item in his outstretched hand, " ...Try one of zese."

Frankie takes the item from the Captain's hand. "Thanks, Cap," he says with a smile.

"Enjoy," says the captain. He looks at Frankie for a moment, shakes his head with affectionate amazement, and then makes his way over to speak with the first lieutenant.

Frankie has no idea what it is, but it's warm. He unwraps the wax paper to discover a freshly baked muffin. Frankie decides that it must have been made especially for the captain, because he's been on that ship for nineteen days and hadn't seen one the whole time. Joao, the producer of the documentary who hired Frankie, comes over to ask if he'd gotten any good footage. "Look what the Captain just gave me," says Frankie showing Joao the muffin. Joao's face lights up when he sees it.

"Man! It's a rice muffin!" Joao exclaims excitedly. "It's an old Portuguese specialty!" he exclaims, as he tears it from Frankie's grasp. He downs half of it before Frankie can blink an eye. "My grandmother used to make these when I was a kid!" he imparts, mouth full, as though it is a significant historical fact, which of course it is. It's the best half a muffin Frankie ever ate.

There are periods when it appears they have passed through the hurricane, but then wham! Back it comes, another five or six hours of horrendous bashing. What knocked Frankie out of his bunk was only the first burst, and it lasted for five hours. After a few days, it becomes clear that they're traveling through the rings of the storm. The satellite image of a hurricane resembles a galaxy in outer space. Both have circular rings that spiral outward from the center. There is a period of eight hours or so in the middle of it all where the sky nearly opens up. The sea continues to rage furiously, but they can almost see blue sky.

Then after that long period, the ferocious storm returns. WHAM! WHAM! WHAM! They had been in the eye of the hurricane, and now must sail through the other side. It is the same thing all over again. The hurricane lasts for five days.

The storm finally dwindles, but the sea continues to roll giant forty-foot swells for days afterward. The light shining through the water, as those high waves roll by, reveals the most beautiful shades of blue Frankie has ever seen. It's exciting adventure all right. Frankie calls it the best five days he's ever spent on planet earth. 'I was wrong...' he thinks. 'There is still great adventure to be found in this world. And this is one of them.' He learns a great lesson on that ship. If he is willing to risk everything and make sacrifices, there are rewards. Great rewards.

It's fair to say that the greatest happiness Frankie has ever known was on that ship, 200 miles out to sea in a hurricane.

XVII

Peyote Road

"Tell me a fact and I'll learn. Tell me a truth and I'll believe. But tell me a story and it will live in my heart forever." Indian Proverb

Not long afterwards, Frankie is invited to teach film production at The School Of Visual Arts in NYC for the summer. At the end of the class, he is hired by one of the adult students to write and direct a documentary about the Comanche Tribe and the Native American Church. The woman who hires him, Berty Bollaney from Dallas, Texas, is a bit loony but somehow endearing. Frankie gladly accepts and flies to Dallas.

Most modern-day Comanche live in or near Lawton, Oklahoma, three and a half hours north of Dallas by car. As part of the gig Berty hires him for, Frankie directs a commercial for Native American jewelry, featuring beautiful Native American women modeling handmade silver and stone creations. They wrap that set in Dallas well after midnight and, as Berty wants Frankie fresh in the morning, she insists that she drive and he try to get some sleep.

Frankie is having a difficult time sleeping because Berty is a terrible driver. Entering I-44 she completely ignores a merge sign, nearly plowing into an 18-wheeler, who blows his horn for a full ten seconds in response.

"Look at these trucks! They just pull out anywhere!" she

exclaims.

"No! The merge sign!?!" Frankie retorts in utter frustration.

He adjusts his seat back as far as it will go. 'If she kills us, at least I'll die in my sleep,' he figures. He manages to get some light napping done. Around 3:00 am, he awakens to Berty fiddling with the radio. Typical North Texas radio which is an assortment of country and Bible stations. She stops on an evangelical preacher from a local station. *"My children, I cannot help but to notice that on Sunday morning some of our parishioners are less than welcoming to our brothers and sisters of color. We must love and embrace all God's children. Remember to read your Bible. The good book will guide you always! It says in Romans: God shall show no favoritism among the races... And if God shall not, then we shall not either"*

Frankie closes his eyes and tries to get a bit more sleep. His thoughts wander to the Plains Indians, and to where he and Berty are traveling. A dreamy image forms in his head. In it he is walking slowly in an orange-colored corridor between a building and a row of trees. There is an Indian man holding an eagle feather walking towards him. The man hands him the feather. He opens his eyes, unsure what the dream is about. Frankie knows that, for the American Indian, even in modern times, the gift of an eagle feather is a great honor made only to those who perform acts of nobility and bravery. Frankie feels it's a self-serving fantasy of something he would love to happen, but doesn't believe he's earned. He gives himself a little speech about it. 'Hey... this isn't about you, man... it's about the Indians. Don't be so self-centered...'

The next morning, after a few hours sleep in a local motel, Berty and he arrive at the Comanche Tribal Complex in Lawton, Oklahoma, where they are to meet with the Chairman to finalize arrangements concerning the documentary. They make their way to the chairman's office and Berty introduces herself. She informs the secretary that she has an appointment with the Chairman, however the secretary is unaware of any such meeting. She checks the calendar out of courtesy and finds nothing on the schedule. Berty insists that she had spoken with the Chairman and that they had agreed to meet. The secretary kindly apologizes for any confusion, and then repeats that there are no meetings on the schedule regarding her. Berty is relentless. Speaking very loudly, she describes in detail her conversation. Unsure as to what might be wrong, Frankie fades into the background and observes the scene from a safe distance. Berty continues to wreak havoc for the ladies in the office as they try to figure out what to do. Things have become very uncomfortable when the Chairman emerges from his office. The expression on his face the moment he recognizes Berty makes it clear that she is perhaps the last person on earth he wants to see.

"Oh! Hello! So good to see you again!" Berty exclaims in a gratuitous excitement, her hand outstretched.

He shakes her hand reluctantly.... "Yes..." he says, grimacing.

"Don't you remember? We met in Fort Worth at the parade..."

"Yes," he repeats, with less enthusiasm than a slug melting in a pool of salt.

"I've been calling for weeks! You're a very hard man to get ahold of!" she says slyly, bordering on flirtatiousness.

"Yes..." comes the less than enthusiastic reply.

The Chairman palms Berty off on the secretary to deal with as she loudly reveals numerous details of what she wants. Frankie remains in the background watching the small commotion that Berty is creating from a safe distance. The Chairman saunters over to join Frankie watch the show. They stand there a moment watching Berty in action when, without turning his head, the Chairman asks, "What are you doing here?"

Frankie looks over to the chairman, who gives Frankie a wry expression.

"I was told you were expecting us and that we were to begin filming a documentary about the Native American Church," Frankie explains.

The Chairman looks Frankie up and down, then with a friendly smile says, "OK, we'll put something together for you."

He arranges for them to conduct several interviews in the Tribunal Court Room as soon as the few hearings scheduled for that morning conclude. "An hour or so..."

he says. Berty keeps the ladies in the office busy as Frankie joins an affable Elder assigned to assist him in anything he might need.

Frankie waits outside the hearing room speaking with the Comanche Elder. He's beginning to feel unsure what exactly he'll be able to accomplish, seeing as their arrival wasn't expected, when two high school aged girls enter the building, wearing denim jackets over Steppenwolf and AC/DC t-shirts. Frankie approaches them and asks if they're members of the Native American Church.

One of the girls speaks up saying, "Yes, I'm a princess and she's a dancer."

Frankie knows the relevance of their titles, and asks if they would like to be in the documentary. They excitedly agree. Although it happened two hundred years ago, being a member of the conquering tribe causes Frankie a degree of unease. He looks down at his feet uncomfortably. "Do you have any Native American regalia?" Frankie asks as politely as he can.

The high school girls look at him bewildered ...silence and fidgeting. The Elder, breaks the tension and says, "He wants to know if you have any of your Injun stuff.

"Oh, yeah! We got Injun stuff!" the girls announce with enthusiasm.

These two wonderful young ladies agree to return with their Native American regalia and illustrate the Gourd Dance (a puberty dance), and the Round Dance (a dance that expresses happiness and joy).

Frankie interviews the Chairman, the Elder, the two high school girls and a few others that first day. A drummer, who was called in to illustrate various drumbeats and explain how they are used, is a big friendly guy with long hair and beads. He is the last interview of the day. Frankie calls a wrap and the Comanche film crew that had been hired for the documentary begins to break down the set.

Frankie approaches the drummer. "Thanks for the drumming," says Frankie, with a smile. They shake hands. "I was going to roll a cigarette... you want one?" Frankie asks.

"Yeah," the drummer answers. They sit down on two crates and Frankie rolls a few cigarettes. Frankie hands the drummer, Kuyani, a hand-rolled smoke. He rolls one for himself and they light up. It occurs to Frankie that they are doing more than just having a cigarette. He and Kuyani are engaged in ritual. The offering and subsequent smoking of tobacco given by a stranger is considered a peaceful and sacred act among the American Indians. Frankie still has a lot to learn.

They speak for a while about the Native American Church. "I was raised in an orphanage," Kuyani tells Frankie. "They made us attend the white man's church," he says. "From what I could see, most people in that church acted like they could do whatever they wanted all week, and as long as they attended church on Sunday, all is good with The Creator."

Frankie listens intently. "In the Native American Church, spirituality is a part of daily life," Kuyani explains. Frankie nods his head.

"I remember the white members of that church treating us as lesser people because we are Indian," Kuyani continued. "And I've read the Bible. It says..."

Frankie interrupts. "In Romans... that God shall show no favoritism among the races," he chimes in, having been given that little gem over the radio the previous night on the drive up. It just came out. He didn't think about it. Kuyani looks over at Frankie...

"Yeah..." he says fondly. They gaze at one another for a moment and time seems to stop.

Kuyani invites Frankie to one day join him and the Elders in sweat lodge. Frankie accepts the gracious invitation. They sit there for a moment talking about the Native American Church and peyote, while smoking the hand-rolled cigarettes as the crew packs up. Frankie notices the beautiful hue of orange light from the setting sun streaming in through the entrance. "Hey, can I make some photographs of you outside in this incredible light?" Frankie asks.

Kuyani peers towards the entrance. "Sure. I have a new poncho and some beads. I'll go get them."

"Great," Frankie answers, "let me get my camera, I'll

meet you out there."

Kuyani walks off to fetch his new poncho and Frankie grabs the Nikon from his camera bag as the crew continues to wrap the set. Frankie steps outside, but doesn't see Kuyani. He looks around and notices a little trail parallel to the building alongside a row of trees and beyond to a secondary parking lot. He walks down the path and spots Kuyani about a thirty yards away, leaning into an old faded green Ford pick-up truck, fiddling with something on the front seat. Kuyani pops his head out of the truck, sees Frankie and walks towards him holding a large eagle feather in his hand.

It is the exact image Frankie had the previous night on the drive up. He tries brushing the image away from view with his hand, blinking repeatedly because he can't believe his own eyes, but it won't go away.

Kuyani reaches Frankie, holds out the large eagle feather and says, "I want you to have this."

Frankie wants to say 'I know', but he can't utter a word. What he thought was a dream or fantasy the night before, was nothing short of a prophetic vision.

Kuyani tells Frankie how, when they called him to ask if he would drum for a documentary film-crew that morning, he had packed the small box of beads and things, that now sits on his front seat. He told Frankie that he'd grabbed the eagle feather not knowing why. He described how it was a mindless act, as though in a dream. He didn't know why he was gathering all that stuff to bring along, he only knew he was supposed to. How his wife had asked him what he was packing all that stuff for, and that he had told her he didn't know, that they needed a drummer at the Complex. She thought his behavior was odd, which it probably was. He tells Frankie that she yelled at him, shook her head, and told him he was crazy. They laugh about it.

"Now I know why I brought the feather," he says, gazing at Frankie with fond affection. Still somewhat speechless, Frankie makes some photographs of Kuyani standing near his truck, and they say their farewell. Frankie returns to the building holding his huge eagle feather. The Comanche film crew stop dead in their tracks, staring at Frankie, with mouths gaped wide.

"Where did you get that?" the cameraman asks.

"Kuyani gave it to me," Frankie tells him. They gather around Frankie in awe of the great occasion.

"Do you understand what an honor it is to be given an eagle feather?" the cameraman asks.

"Yeah... ...I do," is all Frankie can muster.

"I don't even have one," a young Comanche crewmember mutters, looking down at his feet in embarrassment.

The photos are nothing special, but that moment... that moment when Kuyani handed Frankie his eagle feather, will live in his heart forever.

XVIII
The Aftermath

"Something about her was familiar." Harry Chapin

A few decades have passed since the pages chronicled here, and we may never get into all that, but here Frankie is, once again decidedly destitute after a life traveling the world. Often first class on expense accounts, producing everything from television commercials to an award winning Oscar-nominated documentary, feature films, music videos and photo shoots. Pretty much any job in the film industry someone was willing to hire him for. Some things never change... some things aren't meant to...

Frankie has done it all, from producing, writing, and directing to acting, voice-overs and stunts. A famous actor put an ax in his back in a major motion picture once. That could be a chapter all its own.

Then something happens that truly changes his life. He experiences a near fatal accident. Frankie is seriously injured with fractured vertebrae, multiple brain contusions and is rendered comatose. He's in ICU, wearing a neck brace, breathing through a tracheotomy, being given a 50/50 chance to survive by a team of highly skilled neurologists. He's like this for eleven days, when he awakens to see Lady Godiva ride into his room on horseback. She stops and smiles at Frankie for a moment, then rides off into a cloud. He spends 21 days in ICU and those same doctors who had given him a 50/50 chance to live now call him The Miracle Man. From Big Man to The Miracle Man is not a terrible transition, after all is said and done.

When a major life-altering event such as this occurs, the whole show is up for review. Frankie makes a solemn oath to himself in ICU that he will honor who he truly is, and follow his dreams, come what may. Now he needs to take stock and reassess his entire life. He has to find a way to escape the rat race and figure out where to go from here. He must find a respite. A dear friend offers Frankie her decrepit old houseboat in Montauk at the very end of Long Island.

After a few weeks of swimming, fishing and thinking, he becomes listless, spending too much time in his own head. His worst enemy! Since arriving, he's noticed a lot of minivan taxis darting around town. One Saturday afternoon he sees a 'Drivers Wanted' poster at a taxi stand. Larry Darrell from W. Somerset Maugham's 'The Razor's Edge' comes to mind ...Frankie takes it as a sign. So he walks in and inquires about the position. The dispatcher seems overwhelmed and maybe a bit desperate, with the phone ringing off the hook.

"You still need drivers?" Frankie asks.

"Yeah," she says. The phone rings and she answers, "Taxi." She listens for a moment, "Ok, give me ten minutes, honey," she says. She presses the old fashioned desktop microphone and says, "Ten!"

"Ten," comes the voice through the radio.

"Pick up West Lake."

"West Lake Marina... copy," comes the voice over the radio.

The phone rings and she picks up the receiver. "Taxi," she states, with authority. She listens a moment. "Where on the old highway?" She listens and seems frustrated, suddenly. "What's the street address of the closest house then?" She listens... "Ok, then what's the cross street?" She listens for a moment, looks up at Frankie and with her hand over the receiver says, "Unfuckingbelievable!" Into the receiver she says, "Look, honey ...it's a big highway. I can't just send a driver out there looking for a woman standing on the side of the road!" She looks up at Frankie and rolls her eyes as she listens. "I can't send a taxi if you don't know where you are! Find an address or a cross street and call us back!" She slams down the receiver. The phone rings. "Taxi," she listens. "Ok, give me ten minutes." She looks up at Frankie again. The phone rings. She picks up the receiver. "Taxi, please hold." She looks back at Frankie with sheer desperation. You can start now?" she asks.

"Sure," Frankie answers.

"You got a license?" she asks.

"Yes, of course," Frankie answers, reaching for his wallet.

"Forget the license. Show it to me later. You're in number 8!" She hands Frankie a set of keys. "It's in the lot outside. Make sure you've got gas, and turn on the radio," she says, as the phone rings.

Frankie takes the keys. "Taxi. Hold please," he hears as he exits the taxi stand and looks for Taxi number 8.

Frankie thinks it strange that she didn't check his driver's license, but she was slammed and Montauk is a different kind of place. So off he went.

It was a fun, easy job despite the sometimes panicky disposition of the dispatchers and, as Frankie had witnessed, often for justifiable reasons. Montauk is a beautiful and unique place with a gorgeous beach, colorful history, fresh fish, live music and plenty of booze. If you can't find a serene happiness in Montauk, just throw in the towel because your life is about to implode.

Frankie's third day in the taxi he hears the dispatch over the radio. "Eight." "Go for eight," he answers, enjoying the taxi lingo he's learned.

"Pick up dog shit," the dispatcher says, matter of fact, with the same inflection as any other call.

'Whoa!' Frankie thinks. 'I must have pissed somebody off.' It has to be explained to him that Dog Shit Alley is the name locals have given a dirt road off of Fort Pond

Bay, because everyone seemed to have a dog and, well you get it.... she simply shortened the phrase by one word. That old lack of attention to detail can often wreak havoc.

Near the end of the summer, Frankie gets a call for a pickup in Amagansett. He finds the address and pulls up the long wooded driveway to find a large two-story classic Hampton's-style beach house with a huge yard and a cedar fence. He honks the horn. A few moments later, a rather attractive blond woman exits the house and saunters down the driveway towards Frankie, seated in the taxi. Each step she takes triggers a distant synapse in his brain when, finally, a few yards away, as astonishing as it is, it becomes clear to Frankie that it's her. It's Baby Doll. She sticks her head into the passenger side window, looks at Frankie and with matching astonishment says, "Frankie?"

§§§§§

I know what you're probably thinking, but no. Baby Doll landed on her feet. Even had a freckled-face kid. She gave up the life of a high-priced call girl and found her joy raising a family. Frankie was truly happy for her. And as much as there were days deep in Frankie's past when he didn't think it possible, the world kept turning even though they were no longer together.

XIX

Sympathy for the Devil

Long is the way and hard, that out of Hell leads up to light.
John Milton, Paradise Lost
"Thus every dog will have his day – he who this morning smiled, at night
may sorrow; The grub today's a butterfly tomorrow..."
Peter Pindar: Odes of Condolence.

And what a world it is, too! Life is often incredibly mysterious. Sometimes this world is an upside down puzzle turned inside out beyond all reasoning. Beyond all reckoning! Even if you're not Frankie or Baby Doll...

Frankie has changed dramatically these past ten years. He has shifted his primary motivation in life from how to get laid as often as is possible while making a million dollars without actually trying, to seeking true adventure, spreading love and getting to Heaven.

§§§§§

A quiet morning can still find him at The Crossroads talking with his favorite bartender, James.

Frankie refers to a page in his notebook. He looks up at James. "Heaven," he says.

"Heaven," repeats James, dreamfully.

"As it is, who really knows? It's a concept nearly as old as thought itself. Whether or not one believes there's a Heaven, it's a belief that has been and remains frequently misused as a tool for manipulation of the masses by the powers that be, even when the people in positions of power live as though they, themselves, don't believe that there is a Heaven..." He sips his whiskey and looks at James. "They lie about it to stay in power," says Frankie, a bit dismayed.

"Tell me about it," says James pouring himself a Maker's Mark.

Frankie lights a cigarette, turns the page and looks up at James leaning on the bar. "People who believe in the common perception of Heaven are to be envied."

"What an amazing ideal," James comments.

"Of course, if you believe in Heaven, then you must also believe in Hell," Frankie says, taking a sip of whiskey. "One way or another, I suppose everyone grasps the dynamic. Good bad happy sad... it all mirrors Heaven and Hell. But to believe in the old fashioned common perception of Hell... man, fire and brimstone...? What a reality! Better get right with the Big Guy!"

"Or they'll be hell to pay!" James adds.

"Exactly! Which leads us directly to Fear!" Frankie makes a few notes and looks up at James. "Of course, fear isn't any fun whatsoever. It has only limited practical purpose in extreme situations. And if all of us were to simply love one another, most fear could be largely moot, now that dinosaurs are extinct."

"Dinosaurs?" asks James, a bit thrown off.

"I realize it's generally accepted that Man and Dinosaur didn't roam the earth together. However the proponents of that opinion are the same people who insist that we walked out of Africa a hundred thousand years ago, were hunter-gatherers for eighty-five thousand years, just prior to having a synapse one day that allowed us to build the pyramids."

"Must've been some pretty good grass for that kind of synapse to occur," says James with a big grin.

They share a laugh.

"You're right to laugh. Cause even though a third of the population of Texas believes that man and dinosaurs did in fact roam the earth together, and for all we actually know for sure they could be right, it's mainly humor designed to point out that, in this day and age, the primary thing we have to fear on this earth, after God and natural disaster, is each other. Is people!' Frankie says, looking up at James with a sincere expression.

"In any event, Fear undoubtedly leads us to Courage..." Frankie says, following his train of thought.

"To courage," says James, raising his glass.

"To courage," Frankie agrees. They toast.

"Courage is a tool used most often by people of extreme passion ...people driven by love or faith."

James nods his head, thinking...

Frankie looks up at James and then adds... "I say that due to its illogical essence. Courage is a direct result of Fear. When we're full of fear, we can react one of two ways: with courage or cowardice. Without courage... without valor... mankind would not have survived the ages. Our need for courage will always exist. A need that is generated by fear and fear alone," says Frankie, rolling up a cigarette.

"It's been said that discretion is the better part of valor," says James.

"Yes, it has! And that, dear friend ...that leads us to Plan B," Frankie says, taking a sip of his drink.

"We should always have a Plan B," he says. "We should have two in every garage," he adds, smiling.

"But we have cars instead," says James as he fills their glasses.

Frankie chuckles.

"Or is that two chickens in every pot?" asks Frankie. "I suppose that depends on which decade you identify with, and to which race and/or social status you were assigned at birth. For some it might mean something quite different than to others. For instance a..." he pauses a moment, "...oh, I won't say it!" Frankie looks up at James.

"Which leads us to Political Correctness. What a mess!

Hitler would be proud. Next in line would be Pavlov, Freud and anyone ill at ease with the fact that they are Black, White, Red, Yellow, Irish, Bald, Short, Female, Male, Greasy, Missing a Limb, Cripple, Fat, Skinny, Pimply, Deaf, Dumb, Blind, Italian, Catholic, Jewish, Muslim, Protestant, Albino, Non-Humorous Too Humorous or a Stutterer. Perhaps one who has a Big Nose, Small Nose, has a Flat Chest or a Huge Chest, is a Blue-eyed Devil, or is One-eyed, has a Big Head or Too Little a Head, Big Butt, No Butt, Big Dick, Little Dick, Innies, Outies, Black Hair, Blond Hair, Jew, Wasp, Redneck, Damned Yankee, Hick Rebel, White Boy, Chink, Guinea, Wop, Stewardess, Thin Lipped, Fat Lips, Plates in their Lips, OOPS! There I slipped again. Does that comment fall under Too Humorous, Not Humorous, Stereotypical, Racist or Observant with a Satirical Bent?"

"I just don't know," James answers.

"Last time I checked, we, as in 'We the People', lived by and cherished what nowadays appears to be a little-understood premise in America entitled, somewhat cryptically, Free Speech! Not within limits, bounds or good taste, seeing as these are terms left open for much interpretation and manipulation. Free. Say what you will. Speak freely. Open up and let it out, you'll feel better. I promise. In any event, it is evident that Political Correctness, so-called, is first cousin to Fascism," he says.

"Uh oh, hold your tongue," James says, laughing.

"Hehehee... Its impetus may not be overtly fascist, but unfortunately fascism is the sad by-product of political correctness. You can't force people to be nicer toward one other. 'Politically Correct' is a phrase which, in and of itself, has problems, because in its heart of hearts, politics has nothing to do with it. Politics is everything that is wrong with it! What about kindness? Remember that?"

"Kindness," James says, affectionately.

"Or tolerance? Acceptance? Love? Political Correctness is nothing more than a Band-Aid. A remedy based in dishonesty, devised to manipulate or alleviate the symptoms of the maladies in the modern world, but not addressing the disease that causes it. It is an untrue attempt at doing our best to avoid such approaches as 'Hey towel head, which way to the White House?' Which of course brings us to Democracy."

"Democracy..." says James. "There's a famous quote about democracy, but no one really knows who said it first," he adds, sipping his drink.

"Yeah, you're right!" Frankie agrees. "A lot of people are credited with that quote. But I think it was Winston Churchill who first said that Democracy is the worst form of government except all those other forms that have been tried from time to time. Still, Mark Twain phrased it best: 'Democracy is the worst form of government ever invented, except for all the others'."

"To ole Sam Clemens," says James, raising his glass. They toast.

"As much as I love Mark Twain, he may have missed the mark on this one, because in his book 'Common Sense', Thomas Paine calls Democracy 'the most vile form of government ever created'. And he's right too, because America was founded as a Constitutional Republic ruled by law, not on a majority rule based on public opinion that, as we have seen, can be easily manipulated by simple means of mass deception," Frankie says, looking up at James with a suddenly serious expression. He looks at his notes. "Madison warned us of the inherent dangers of democracies with these words, 'Democracies have ever been spectacles of turbulence and contention; have ever been found incompatible with personal security or the rights of property; and have in general been as short in their lives as they have been violent in their deaths...' "Which I believe, and I don't think I'm wrong, brings us to Despair," he says, taking a long swig of whiskey.

"I find despair, true despair, not melodramatic or even personal despair, such solemn territory that I must rely on men of letters far greater than myself in what must surely be a vain attempt to grasp in words." Frankie flips a few pages in his notebook. "I wrote some great quotes about it in here somewhere," He finds the page he's looking for and reads aloud.

'*Never despair; but if you do, work on in despair.*' Edmund Burke. I must have a dozen of his quotes here somewhere.

Albert Camus wrote, '*He who despairs over an event is a coward, but he who holds hope for the human condition is a fool.*'

Here's one from George Bernard Shaw. '*He who has never hoped can never despair.*'

Joseph Conrad wrote, '*I can't tell if a straw ever saved a drowning man, but I know that a mere glance is enough to make despair pause. For in truth we who are creatures of impulse are creatures of despair.*'

"Phew! Conrad..." says James.

Kahlil Gibran said '*Tenderness and kindness are not signs of weakness and despair, but manifestations of strength and resolution.*'

"The Prophet... great book," James states, raising his glass.

"Man, you're venturing into some solemn territory," he adds, sipping his whiskey.

Frankie looks up at James with a wry, bittersweet smile.

"Solemn territory perhaps, but common territory nonetheless," Frankie says, pausing a moment in thought. "More than at any other time in history, mankind faces a crossroads. One path leads to utter despair and hopelessness, the other to total extinction. Maybe there's a third path. Let us pray we have the wisdom to choose correctly," he says, a tear in his eye.

XX

Heaven's Gate

"And I can't be running back and forth forever between grief and high delight." - J. D. Salinger

"For after all, the best thing one can do when it is raining is let it rain." - Henry Wadsworth Longfellow

Frankie hasn't experienced the level of despair as portrayed in many of the previous chapters for a very long time. It's clear to him now that, when living as a heroin addict, he minimized his problems into one ball of wax: Getting straight. Junkies have to maintain their addiction with daily doses of heroin or they begin to jones (experience withdrawal symptoms). Most junkies refer to these bags as maintenance bags. In order for a junkie to get high, in the common sense of what it means to get high, he has to fix enough dope to surpass the amount required to satisfy his addiction. As a result, for the most part, junkies get 'straight'. When you're addicted to heroin and you need a fix, not having one is nothing short of agonizing. You have to get straight! And once you are, not a thing in the world can touch you. You haven't a care in the world. You have no problems concerning romance, bills to pay, bad weather or rent. You certainly don't have any aches and pains. If you're a photographer, your photographs are better. If watching television, Gilligan's Island can be downright philosophical. When you're riding 'the horse', life is good. It's that simple. Perhaps the word 'life' in that sentence is too kind. But what else would you call it? A delightfully distorted perception of life might be more accurate...

Heroin works wonders in alleviating any and all problems of the day. What is it about certain people? What makes them junkies? Addictions range from passionate love of chocolate to heroin, and everything in between. But, certainly, heroin is in a class all its own. You can bet your ass they weren't handing out Hershey bars to the injured on the battlefields of the Civil War! Or WWI and WWII for that matter. Morphine - heroin - essentially the same. The difference being one step of refinement from the same source: papaver somniferum, the opium poppy.

As much as it can be said that for the most part junkies are pitiable people, in a class of their own, mankind leads a less than natural life in the modern industrialized world. Most people exist outside the rhythms of nature and ultra-sensitive souls often pursue misguided solutions, like using heroin, attempting to reconnect deep-seated instinctual aspects of life that have been severed.

Consider the religious practices of the Plains Indians ...the fact that, at the advent of the imposed reservation period in the history of the American Indian of the Southwest, they choose to adopt the consumption of peyote as a Holy Sacrament to be a part of their spiritual practice. And it's a religion that lives on to this day. True, peyote isn't addictive, far from it. American Indians call it 'medicine', and that's just what it is, and is known to have cured all manner of disease.

It is a curious fact that, prior to the American Indian being stripped of freedom, when they were still able to nourish a natural relationship with the earth, they found no need for peyote to sustain a divine spiritual connection to the Creator, to God. Yet, at the precise chronological moment in history that the American Indian is relegated to an existence in near captivity preventing them from living a natural life, they adopt, in large numbers, a practice foreign to them, indigenous to the Huichol, Tarahumara and other Indian Tribes along the Rio Grande and in the Chihuan Valley of Mexico where peyote grows naturally and is believed by some academics and laymen alike to have a history of use stretching back twenty-five thousand years. Is it possible that ingesting peyote creates an induced spiritual connection to the spirit world that previously had been attained through the practice of a certain knowledge and belief system of a ceremonial life in a natural setting? In large part, through wisdom gained from challenging and overcoming one's fears and a nurturing of faith in the unknown? Is there a parallel on a fundamental level?

Heroin alleviates even the most severe pains. However this is a temporary solution and is not intended to replace conquest and achievement as methods of survival. Heroin is a religion all its own. Religion isn't the opiate of the masses, opium is, and always has been. Nearly all religion, practiced truthfully and faithfully, even as imperfect as each one might be, when pursued with full heart in earnest sacrificial love, can be a path to the truth of God: to Wisdom. And with wisdom comes peace.

§§§§§

Whether God exists or does not exist cannot be proven or disproven. Believing or not believing in a Supreme Being requires a blind belief either way.

As much as this is a two-millennia-long discussion, if you choose to not believe in the existence of God, the question is why? There is no more proof that God does not exist than that He does. Deciding to not believe in God requires an equal degree of rash conviction as deciding to believe that God does exist. Considering that we must all possess a belief that cannot be proven, or live in utter doubt, why shouldn't we choose something hopeful? The price for the answer to the age-old question of whether or not God actually exists is our life, because expiring from this dimension is the only way to unravel that mystery. If the faithful are wrong, what exactly will they have lost? Time in prayerful contemplation wasted that they might have spent at a ballgame ...or an orgy? If those without faith in God are wrong, when they die the consequences are likely to be far more severe. As ironic as it may sound, weighing the cost involved for each proposition, believing God exists is actually the more logical solution.

It is interesting to note that some of the greatest minds in the history of mankind put their faith in a Supreme Being.

Albert Einstein, who of course is one of the most highly recognized and revered scientists of the twentieth century, was very clear about his belief in the existence of God. Born in 1879 in the German Empire to Jewish parents, Einstein for the most part lived his adult life as a secular Jew. Yet, he was not an atheist, as is often suggested. The founder of modern physics and Nobel laureate expressed the impossibility of a non-created universe, saying, 'Everyone who is seriously committed to the cultivation of science becomes convinced that in all the laws of the universe is manifest a Spirit vastly superior to man, and to which we with our powers must feel humble.' He wrote that he had 'a humble admiration of an infinitely superior Spirit that reveals itself in the little that we, with our weak and transitory understanding, can comprehend.' According to Max Jammer, who was a personal friend of Einstein and a professor of physics, "Einstein always protested against being regarded as an atheist." Einstein insisted that, "A legitimate conflict between science and religion cannot exist. Science without religion is lame; religion without science is blind."

Einstein's hero, Sir Isaac Newton, upon whose work nearly all of classical physics is built, was a deeply religious Christian. He saw the hand of God in everything. For Newton, all of the great laws of physics that he discovered were the laws of God that testified to His design. He would very likely be dismayed to know that, centuries later, atheists claim that he had really only discovered self-existent laws, which explain the universe so well that God is no longer needed in the equation. Newton wrote a book published in 1733 that few have ever heard of entitled 'Observations on the Prophecies of Daniel and the Apocalypse of St. John'. His insights vary to some extent from many of the standard modern Christian interpretations, but his prescience might yet be vindicated, as many of these prophecies are yet to be fulfilled. He is quoted as saying, 'What we know is a drop, what we do not know is a vast ocean. The admirable arrangement and harmony of the universe could only have come from the plan of an omniscient and omnipotent being.'

Maria Mitchell, America's first female astronomer, and the first woman to be named to the American Academy of Arts and Sciences was born into a Quaker family. In her twenties, she began to question her denomination's teachings, and was eventually disbarred from membership for the rest of her life. Maria was a religious seeker who pursued a simpler type of faith. After hearing a minister preach about the dangers of science, Mitchell wrote, 'Scientific investigations, pushed on and on, will reveal new ways in which God works, and bring us deeper revelations of the wholly unknown.'

There are many more famous scientists, including one in three living today, who share the belief in God. Nearly fifty are Nobel Laureates. And are Christian, Jew and Muslim.

The old Stuart Chase quote rings true... 'For those who believe, no proof is necessary. For those who don't believe, no proof is possible.' Whether you believe in God or not, it is entirely understandable how so many people have become resentful of religion. Especially when religion is so often used as a front. A con. Most religions have long been and continue to be wrongly used as a means of manipulation of entire populations by various powers that be, their true meanings lost in a sea of grief. And yes, more people have been killed in the name of God than for any other reason, but that is not God's fault. If we were to, in earnest, live by the laws Moses told us were given to him directly by God, and by the wisdom contained in the many parables of Jesus, this world would be a totally different place right now. God gave us a choice a long time ago. We have free will. It is our hands that have shaped the world we live in ...and what a fucking mess we've made of it!

§§§§§

Frankie has subdued most of his demons and is determined to live a life of adventure, filled with wisdom and love. He attempts to spread love wherever he goes. His life is far from trouble free, but not running away from hard times is proving to be far better than having a monkey on his back.

"Expectations have often proven deadly, in my experience," he says, rolling a cigarette. "But hope springs eternal and I refuse to succumb to the treachery of this world. I would rather be disappointed than undone." He lights the cigarette and smiles. "It's not easy being me, but it's worth it!" he adds, "And even though the Garden of Eden we began with is presently little more than an outcropping of weeds, living in this magic-filled place we call Planet Earth is still more than worth the price of admission, and always has been ...if we're smart enough to see it that way. Notwithstanding the fact that the uttermost vile and evil people in the world think they own it; bankers! Yeah, you pricks might want to consider that you can't take it with you!" Frankie says, with a wink and a shake of the head. "In spite of all that the human race has lost, and of the treacherous forces that rule the world ...that create struggle and mayhem for the rest of us... I've come to realize that sometimes there are no solutions to our problems. Sometimes we are obliged to pray and white-knuckle our way through them. That, although people are frequently selfish and often mistaken, we must embrace them with love and forgive them, realizing that we, too, are frequently selfish and often mistaken. That anger and violence are rarely justified. That our survival instincts can run amok, far exceeding their intended purpose, and evolve into obsessions, driving us towards destruction ...dominating us to the point where they eventually rule our lives. That basically, I'm just another guy with all the same problems of all the other guys in the world ...and lucky to have them." Then he just smiled and strolled off like a man without a care in the world.

Finis

ABOUT THE AUTHOR

New York-born French-Italian writer Peter Bové is a naturally prolific creator from whom work spills out with incredible frequency and range. A poet and fine artist from an early age, he is also a musician and composer, a novelist, a screenwriter, filmmaker, actor and performer – as well as philosopher, astronomer and carpenter. He began his career studying fine art at The New School in New York City where he delved into myriad art forms, eventually exploring performance art, theater and film. This voyage of discovery led to a long and successful career in entertainment and commercial media, however never diminishing his passion for painting and drawing or the written word. Over the years, he has continued to produce written and fine art pieces, which he is now working to bring to the public eye. Mr. Bové has always been motivated and inspired by love and faith in opposition to the misery and corrupted ideals of the world we live in. This underlying theme is reflected throughout all of his compositions and the resolution of this conflict continues to be the beacon that guides his artistic journey. When he's not in Montauk Mr. Bové lives in Dallas, Texas, on a hill, where he can get a good view of the stars and bring them down to earth with paper, canvas, paint and the mighty pen.

49702825R00154

Made in the USA
Middletown, DE
22 June 2019